'Being "married" to Joanna Lumley has been a complete joy Roger Allam

'Jan Etherington has the pen of an angel … she is a brilliant writer and these books are sheer joy. Bravi tutti!' Joanna Lumley

'This book gives me hope that life and marriage might permanently include taking the absolute piss while simultaneously dancing in the kitchen' Emma Freud

'Comedies about likeable people are not common. Treasure this one' *Sunday Times*

'Sitcom is what most marriages are really like – repetitive and ridiculous – and Jan's words are some of the best ever written on the subject …' Richard Curtis

'An endearing portrait of exasperation, laced with hard won tolerance – and love' *Guardian*

'This warm, witty portrait of a forty-year marriage is written with a pin-sharp perception. Sublimely funny, touching … couple Joanna and Roger remain passionate about life, music and each other, as their conversations veer from reading glasses and dodgy knees to clubbing in Ibiza, separate beds and affairs. Joanna Lumley and Roger Allam have had illustrious acting careers but can they ever have done anything better than Jan Etherington's two hander? A funny, relatable read … this is a work of supreme craftsmanship' *Radio Times*

'One of the best writers for radio ... Her dialogue works because it is so true' Simon Brett

'Beautifully written' *Observer*

'Astute ... They are unlike anyone I actually know [and], I truly like them' *The Times*

'*Conversations from a Long Marriage* is a brilliant vehicle for tackling difficult subjects, like ageing and mortality, with a kind of clever, gentle, sardonic and affectionate humour, laced with human insight that makes you chuckle but can also unexpectedly move you' *Suffolk Magazine*

'Witty and warm' *Spectator*

'The delicious fruit of the writer, Jan Etherington's experience of writing lots of TV and radio, blessed by being acted by Joanna Lumley and Roger Allam. This series makes people laugh' Gillian Reynolds

'Not just comedy but also a compelling, well-rounded drama. Brilliantly crafted, delightfully funny and perceptive ... they sparkle and spring vividly to life' *Mature Times*

'Pin-sharp' *Lady*

'Exquisitely simple ... it captures the rhymes and language of spousal life [and] in [Jan Etherington's] hands it works perfectly' Ben Dowell, *The Times* Pick of the Week

'The beloved couple ... whose flirty, combative relationship made famous by Joanna Lumley and Roger Allam ... is beautifully captured in Etherington's sparkling dialogue' Simon O'Hagan, *i* newspaper

Conversations from a Long Marriage

Jan Etherington

SOUVENIR
PRESS

This paperback edition published in 2023
First published in Great Britain in 2022 by
Souvenir Press,
an imprint of Profile Books Ltd
29 Cloth Fair
London
ECIA 7JQ
www.souvenirpress.co.uk

First performed on BBC Radio 4
Conversations from a Long Marriage scripts copyright © Jan Etherington,
pilot 2018, series one 2020, series two 2021

Design by Crow Books

1 3 5 7 9 10 8 6 4 2

Printed and bound in Great Britain by
CPI Group (UK) Ltd, Croydon, CRO 4YY

ISBN 978 1 80081 2406
eISBN 978 1 80081 2413

For GAVIN
Still my hot date, after forty years

Author's Note

The idea for my comedy *Conversations from a Long Marriage* was born, bizarrely, out of fury. I was angry about the way older women were portrayed in drama and comedy. Either as miserably married interfering mothers-in-law, bitter ex-wives, tetchy, spiteful control freaks – or as technophobic grannies in pinnies, patronised by the whole family.

'Come on!' I'd shout at my radio and TV. 'Where are my contemporaries? The strong, smart, funny women who have laughed and loved their way through life since the Summer of Love and might still be married to the sexy hippy they met at Glastonbury '71?'

We may be Senior Railcard holders but we turn up the car radio, sing along with Marvin Gaye and are still dancing in the street with Martha and the Vandellas. Yet we were nowhere represented. So I wrote a series myself, about a woman who I recognised, who had my references. I placed her in a long marriage that still fizzed with passion for life, music, wine and, yes, sex – and I knew who I wanted to play her.

Joanna Lumley epitomises how we all want to grow older. Not just beautiful but engaged, curious, warm, clever and funny. Thank God she said yes, because I didn't have a back-up choice! I knew who I wanted to play her husband. I told Joanna and held my breath. 'Roger Allam?! I'm in!'

Joanna said. 'He's a sensational actor, with one of the best voices in broadcasting!' Hurrah! My Dream Team was born!

In 2017, we recorded a pilot episode and when I first saw those two at the microphone, I couldn't stop smiling. I have a schoolgirl crush on them both – as do many of the listeners. Their chemistry was obvious; they genuinely like each other. There is much banter, flirting and laughter in the studio – and that's before we even start – but our calm and confident producer, Claire Jones, miraculously manages to pull it all together.

I always planned *Conversations from a Long Marriage* as a two-hander, about a couple talking when no one else can hear. There are the occasional one-sided phone chats but no other characters and definitely no neighbours bursting in, uninvited. It's sometimes mundane, as they bicker about the bins, dishwasher loading and the etiquette of waving goodbye at the front door, but scattered through the eighteen episodes of the three series so far, we learn their history. A tragic miscarriage soon after they met has left them childless, they have each taken detours off the marital motorway – split up, come back together – and even now, there are jealousies and dramas which fuel the passion and the humour.

I wanted the series to be optimistic, aspirational, warm and funny. The responses have been extraordinary. One listener said, 'It makes me want to work harder at my own marriage.' Another said, 'You say this is about older people but I've had this conversation with my girlfriend this morning,' and a young couple told me, 'We're newly married but what is so encouraging is that these two have obviously been through separations, crises and lived apart and yet love and passion have survived. That's very heartening to know, when so many give up too easily on marriage.'

I've been writing comedy for over thirty-five years, often with my husband, Gavin Petrie. We were both journalists when we submitted our first script to the *Radio Times* 'Sounds Funny' competition in 1987. The judges were Victoria Wood, Prunella Scales and Douglas Adams (creator of *The Hitchhiker's Guide to the Galaxy*). We won! The prize was £2,000, which we spent on a stair carpet and a juicer. As Gavin was then Features Editor of *RT*'s rival, *TV Times*, it provided a lot of merriment.

Gavin and I have written many more radio and TV series together and although I wrote *Conversations from a Long Marriage* on my own, I asked Gavin's advice and opinion. 'What do you think is the secret of a long, happy marriage?' He answered swiftly, 'You tell me and I'll agree.' That made me laugh – which is probably why we're still together.

Do I draw on my own marriage for ideas? Of course – but everyone else's as well. It's also a work of imagination, inspired by the magical pairing of Joanna and Roger, their speech rhythms and, sometimes, their own observations about marriage. Roger and I have discussed the ritual of 'non-drinking days' and Joanna told me, 'You've been listening at my window, Jan,' when she read the first episode, about how ageing is so infuriating because you feel the same inside.

Choosing a favourite episode would be like choosing

a favourite child, but perhaps the episodes where they are revisiting their past or facing their own mortality when a good friend dies have an added poignancy. Sometimes, I end up in tears when I'm writing!

I'm thrilled at the ecstatic reception to *Conversations* from both critics and listeners – and now readers. And I'd like to share with you one final, very important thing I've learned from this show: when a photo is being taken, never, *ever* stand next to Joanna Lumley.

Jan Etherington, 2022

So? Cappuccino? Flat White? Latte? Oatmilk Double Decaff Dishwater? What do you want to DRINK!!? Love you xx

Answer me! I'm in the queue at the counter and ... Too late. Bye!

Where are you? I'm bored. Hurry up. Place is heaving. If you can't see me, do not whistle when you come in. I am not a Labrador. Still love you. Just! xx

It's in His Kiss

The Shoop Shoop Song (It's in His Kiss) – Cher

SCENE 1: *Café. Roger is just paying for two coffees at the café counter when Joanna approaches*

Roger   Hi. I've got you a latte with an extra shot.

Joanna Oh, OK.

Roger   What's wrong with that?

Joanna Nothing. I fancied a cappuccino, that's all.

Roger   I knew it. Even when I think I've got it right, I haven't.

Joanna A latte is fine. Where are we sitting?

Roger   Wherever you say. I would never choose a table without your approval.

Joanna This one's fine.

Roger   Are you absolutely certain it ticks all the boxes? Right position, away from the loos, no small children nearby …

Joanna [*laughs*] Stop it! Although maybe over there …

Roger sighs.

Joanna I'm joking.

6

A clatter as chairs are pulled back, cups are put down and they sit down.

Joanna So. What do you think?

Roger I think this place is going downhill. They used to clean the tables immediately. I mean, look at this! Have you got a wet wipe?

Joanna I'm not talking about the café!

Roger No?

Joanna Notice anything different about me?

Silence.

Roger Oh, I hate it when you do that! Last time you'd had your eyebrows threaded. That was pretty obscure.

Joanna Well, this time it's obvious!

Roger You've had your hair cut! I like it that length.

Joanna I'm not having it cut till Friday.

Roger So … it's …

Joanna Look at my face.

Roger I am.

Joanna I'm wearing glasses! How could you miss that?

Roger Well, of course I knew about the glasses. I thought you meant something else.

Joanna Why would I mean something else?

Roger Because the glasses aren't a surprise. I knew you were getting the glasses …

Joanna You didn't actually know that I was picking them up today because I didn't expect them to be ready. But I popped in on the off chance – and they were there.

Roger So I see. Good.

Joanna What do you think?

7

Roger   They're fine.

Joanna Fine is a weather forecast – not a compliment!

Roger   You want a compliment? OK. You look very nice. But …

Joanna But?

Roger   But … different.

Joanna Funny that you didn't notice I look *different* till now. And what does different mean?

Roger   It means … it makes you look quite … serious … purposeful.

Joanna You hate them.

Roger   No. I don't. They make you look like someone to be reckoned with. Tough.

Joanna Not sexy, then?

Roger   [*an instinctive reaction*] God, no! I mean … Yes! If you like the Miss Discipline look. Which I'm quite keen on. Fortunately.

Joanna So are you saying I look like a social worker or Miss Whiplash?

Roger   I'm not saying anything else at all. Just drink your coffee.

A small pause while she takes a sip of coffee.

Joanna I hate them, too.

Roger   I didn't say I hated them. I'll get used to them and so will you.

Joanna I don't think I even need them.

Roger   Well, you do. You're having trouble night driving … But you resent them. That's why you're being so incredibly snippy.

Joanna   No. Shall I tell you why I'm being snippy? Because I went up to the reception at the optician and this … twelve-year-old bellowed out in a ship-launching voice, 'Date of birth?' I suggested I give him my address instead but he said it's company policy. Can you believe it? The company actually has a policy of shouting people's ages across the shop!

Roger   I'm sure they'll be reviewing it after your visit.

Joanna   I told him I'd write it down –

Roger   A reasonable compromise.

Joanna   – so I did and he said, 'Wow! You certainly don't look that old!'

Roger   Which is a compliment.

Joanna   No, it's patronising and he said that out loud so that everyone knows I am quite old.

Roger   Did you call for the manager?

Joanna   Obviously not. I don't want to start discussing my age in front of everyone.

Roger   OK. You've just had a bit of a life-marker moment.

Joanna   Is that what it's called?

Roger   One of those 'firsts' that come with age. Remember when you got all doomy when you found your first grey hair and dived head first into a bowl of jet-black dye?

Joanna   And you called me Morticia for a month, which was cruel.

Roger   But spot on. You always said my honesty was one of the things you loved about me.

Joanna	That was in the early days when you only said nice things.
Roger	I've been quite nice about your first trifocals.
Joanna	What's next? My first mobility scooter?
Roger	Think of it this way. We're lucky: we've got the chance to get older together.
Joanna	Really?
Roger	Well, what's the alternative?
Joanna	Divorce?
Roger	No! *Not* getting older ... shuffling off this mortal coil, pushing up daisies, joining the choir invisible ...
Joanna	Are you going to do the entire parrot sketch?
Roger	Oh, cheer up!
Joanna	That's the most depressing phrase in the English language.
Roger	Look, why don't we go to the bedding department at Barrett's?
Joanna	Why?
Roger	Fondling their 800-thread-count Egyptian cotton sheets never fails to lift your spirits. Or we could dent their memory mattresses ...
Joanna	Actually, I would like to check out their single beds.
Roger	[*appalled*] What? Why?
Joanna	A very high percentage of married couples sleep in separate rooms, y'know.
Roger	Who do we know who does?
Joanna	Sally and Peter.
Roger	Obviously. They've split up.
Joanna	Yes but they've slept apart for a while.

Roger	Maybe that's why he had an affair. If she wasn't … y'know … up for it.
Joanna	I can't believe you said that! They slept apart because of his deafening snoring!
Roger	She could have just thumped him, like you do with me.
Joanna	He snored through the thumps. But Sally said now he's left, she's getting a decent night's sleep. She's trying to be positive about the break-up.
Roger	Good. Maybe she's turned a corner.
Joanna	You'd be the first to know. Sally is always phoning you up.
Roger	She's labouring under the delusion that Peter talks to me.
Joanna	And you don't disillusion her?
Roger	No.
Joanna	Because you're flattered that an attractive woman chooses you as her confidant?
Roger	Yes.
Joanna	Right. Single beds it is.
Roger	I wouldn't like to sleep on my own all the time.
Joanna	But it's nice to have … options. I like having the bed to myself now and then.
Roger	Me too. If you've got a cold, or restless legs …
Joanna	Or we've had a row …
Roger	And you huff off to the spare room, I sleep fantastically well.
Joanna	I know. I can hear you snoring. With both doors shut.

Roger   There's a theory that single beds are more romantic. Because you can visit each other in the night. Creep in, like illicit lovers.

Joanna   But you've never done that, have you?

Roger   I aim to disappoint.

They laugh. Joanna scrapes back her chair.

Joanna   Oh, quick! That window table's free!

Roger   I thought you were happy with this one.

Joanna   You know me better than that. Hurry up!

Roger   Just once it would be nice to have a coffee without changing tables.

Joanna calls back at him.

Joanna   Come on! Bring the cups!

They move tables. Sit down.

Joanna   That's better.

Roger   [*astounded*] Is it? *Why?!*

She looks out of the window.

Joanna   Look at those two, by the bus stop. I bet they're not talking about single beds. Those early days of passion, when you're welded together with lust … We used to be just like that.

Roger   No we didn't. I'd never wear brown shoes with jeans.

Joanna   These horrible glasses keep slipping down. Do they look straight?

Roger   Yes. But that's enough about you! How am I?

Joanna   Oh, sorry. How did your check-up go?

Roger   Blood pressure OK. The pills are working. But definitely need a knee op.

Joanna   Did you ask him about your memory?

Roger   No. You know what it's like, bit of a rush. Doctor's busy.

Joanna   I don't think you asked him because you don't think it's a problem.

Roger   You're right.

Joanna   But you have trouble remembering things. You used to be sharper.

Roger   So did you.

Joanna   Nothing wrong with my brain. I do crosswords and watch *University Challenge*. You have to exercise the brain like any other part of your body.

Roger   Are you quoting from an NHS pamphlet? You'll be asking me next how many units I drink.

Joanna   I know exactly. Too many. I think we should have at least two days a week without alcohol.

Roger   Those glasses are definitely making you bossier.

Joanna   *And* I think we should go for a really long walk at least twice a week.

Roger   In opposite directions?

Joanna   Since Bonzo Dog died, we haven't been on long walks. I miss walking with a purpose. Don't you?

Roger   No. I'm in favour of aimless ambling. Do you want another coffee?

Joanna   Better not.

Roger   Why? Is coffee bad for you as well?

Joanna   No, coffee's quite good. In moderation.

Roger   I hate that word. Moderation.

Joanna It just means be sensible. Which is a good idea.

Roger Can you hear yourself? You threw a plate of spaghetti at me once for saying you were sensible. You said it was a huge insult.

Joanna It was. It is. Oh, I don't know. I'm just in a bad mood. It's intimations of mortality.

Roger Oh, good. For once, it's not my fault.

Joanna drains her coffee.

Joanna I'm off.

Roger Where're you going?

Joanna I've got to be at the dentist in ten minutes.

Roger Of course. I forgot.

Joanna You see? That's what I'm saying. You definitely need to train your memory.

Roger Right. Take those glasses off!

Joanna takes them off.

Joanna OK. Why?

Roger Oh, Miss Moneypenny. You're ravishing!

Joanna Why do you always try to change the subject with a joke?

Roger Put them back on. I thought maybe the glasses were making you so tetchy but no, it's just you.

Joanna Thank you. Now, I'm off to another lecture on flossing and gum recession. My gums used to be even. Now they're like the Swiss Alps. Why aren't yours? You don't even floss!

Roger Well, obviously, flossing is what's causing the problem. It's not natural, rubbing string between your teeth. And not necessary. See?

Joanna Shut your mouth. I don't want to see your perfect gums.

Roger Did you say I was perfect?

Joanna Just your gums. See you later.

Roger Do you want me to wait for you?

Joanna Well, you've got the car …

Roger I know but I thought I might walk home.

Joanna Good. Walk briskly and swing your arms.

Roger I'm not doing it to keep fit. It's so I don't have to go home with you.

Joanna If you're walking, could you stop by the post office and get a dozen first-class stamps?

Roger Right.

Joanna Oh and we need some dishwasher salt …

Roger Two things? That's a shopping trip!

Joanna No. A shopping trip is a loaded trolley – and the dry cleaning.

Roger But I'm walking.

Joanna Exactly. And you can get them both in the precinct.

Roger I might fancy going through the park.

Joanna Well, don't.

Roger But if I'm getting shopping, I'll have to carry it all.

Joanna Stamps aren't heavy.

Roger Dishwasher salt is. Can't you get them?

Joanna No!

Roger Well, I'd better get going then, if I've got all this shopping to do!

He stands up.

Joanna Fine. I'll take the car home, then.

She stands up.

Roger What are you waiting for?

Joanna You have the car keys!

Roger Oh, sorry …

Joanna You forgot?

Roger All right, Miss Point Scorer.

He hands over the car keys.

Joanna Bye!

Roger Hang on, you *forgot* to ask me where the car's parked. Admit it!

Joanna Oh, I'm sure you're loving this.

Roger Very much indeed.

MUSIC BREAK

The Shoop Shoop Song – Cher

SCENE 2: *The kitchen at their house. Joanna is stirring soup. Roger enters with no shopping bag.*

Roger Mmmm … Minestrone. You've been busy.

Joanna No I haven't. Defrosted it. Not quite ready. What've you been doing? I thought you'd be home ages before me.

Roger I had to get all this shopping, remember?

Joanna [*laughs*] That must have taken seconds.

Roger Here's the stamps.

Joanna turns as he takes them out of his pocket and puts them on the table.

Joanna   Second class? We never buy second-class stamps. I
         wanted first class.

Roger   There was a queue in the post office, so I got
         them at the newsagent's. I used my initiative.
         Found an alternative supplier. But that's all they
         had.

*He reaches in the other pocket and takes out a small packet of
dishwasher salt.*

Joanna   And what's that?

Roger   What does it look like?

Joanna   It looks like a giveaway sample of dishwasher salt.
         I didn't know they sold it in such small amounts.

Roger   Well, now you've learned something.

Joanna   Why didn't you get a normal size?

Roger   Because I had to carry it. I didn't fancy staggering
         down the street with fifteen kilos of salt on my
         back.

Joanna   This won't even make the light go out.

Roger   The what?

Joanna   The 'out of salt' warning light. This titchy little
         trickle is not going to register.

Roger   You asked for stamps and dishwasher salt. I got
         what you wanted.

Joanna   You didn't. You got a sample of what I wanted,
         in both cases. I'll have to go and get some more
         tomorrow.

Roger   You wouldn't want it any other way.

Joanna   It wasn't a lot to ask, was it?

Roger   Just accept that you're married to a man who

	never quite gets it right. It'll stop you being continually disappointed.
Joanna	Call me an optimist but I still believe one day you'll come home with the right kind of bread.
Roger	I can't be brilliant at everything but I do have astounding observational skills. I notice, for instance, you're not wearing the new glasses. Where are they?
Joanna	I've put them down somewhere …
Roger	Aren't you supposed to wear them all the time?
Joanna	No. Just for driving, reading, TV, crosswords, computers, cooking …
Roger	You should put them on one of those gold chains.
Joanna	I'll pretend you didn't say that.
Roger	I'm sure there's a Track My Glasses app for your phone. If you could find your glasses, you could look it up. Or, here's another possibility …
Joanna	What?
Roger	Maybe you really want to lose them. You deliberately can't find your glasses because you hate them.
Joanna	That doesn't even make sense and anyway, it's not true because I really love my new glasses now.
Roger	Marvellous. That didn't take long. So you had no problems driving home in them?
Joanna	Quite the reverse. It was very … enlightening.
Roger	Oh, good.
Joanna	I didn't realise how much my eyes had deteriorated. I used to walk along without really

noticing things. They were sometimes a bit blurry, if I'm honest.

Roger   [*genuinely pleased*] I'm happy that you can see things so clearly now.

Joanna   Oh, I can. As I was driving, everything was much brighter, properly in focus …

Roger   That's a result, then.

Joanna   I saw a lot of people I knew. Including you.

Roger   Me?

Joanna   And Sally. Together.

Roger   When?

Joanna   I was driving down Castle Street. On my way home.

Roger   Why didn't you pick me up?

Joanna   I actually thought of running you over.

Roger   What have I done now?

Joanna   I saw you kiss Sally.

Roger   She kissed me!

Joanna   Oh, the instant response of the obviously guilty!

Roger   I'm not guilty of anything!

Joanna   Snogging Sally?

Roger   It wasn't a snog. It was a peck. On the cheek. We all do it. In fact, you started it. I never used to kiss friends. You made me. You said I was stand-offish.

Joanna   There's a difference between an air-kiss and … you were entwined!

Roger   She got her earring caught in my sweater. Look, here's where the thread was pulled.

Joanna   Convenient.

Roger Oh, for goodness' sake! I just bumped into her and we had a chat.

Joanna What about?

Roger I said I'd booked a hotel room for Friday and could she ask for Mr Smith at the desk.

Joanna Hilarious. It's odd. That you didn't come in and say you'd met Sally straight away. I waited for you to say it. But obviously, you didn't want to tell me.

Roger Give me a chance. I had to unload all this shopping!

Joanna So you can't speak while you put six stamps on the table?

Roger OK. Well, I also saw Terry, Val and her cockerpoo, the bloke who comes round with the fish and Brian's dad. It's a very small town. Do you want a list of everyone I met?

Joanna Only the ones you snogged.

Roger Oh, I saw Peter as well!

Joanna Where?

Roger Outside the post office, just after I left you.

Joanna Why didn't you tell me?

Roger I forgot … I just remembered.

Joanna How did he look?

Roger Like … Peter.

Joanna Did he look guilty?

Roger What does guilty look like?

Joanna Shifty. You know, pretending not to see you.

Roger No, he smiled. Raised a manly arm in greeting. So did I. We went our separate ways.

Joanna   Didn't you speak to him?!

Roger   Why would I speak to him?

Joanna   Because you know him!

Roger   And I acknowledged that fact – and moved on.

Joanna   Didn't you ask him how he was?

Roger   No.

Joanna   Why not?!

Roger   Because he would have thought I was barmy.

Joanna   It's a perfectly reasonable question.

Roger   Oh, if you'd seen Sally, I'm sure you would have
          run across the road, arms outstretched. Big hug.
          Concerned expression. 'How have you been? I've
          been worried about you ...'

Joanna   Course. That's normal.

Roger   It most definitely isn't for blokes. We respect each
          other's privacy. We do not pry. We do not tell
          another bloke his hair looks nice, or ask him if
          he's lost weight ...

Joanna   I don't see why it should be any different for men
          or women. If you care about your friends—

Roger   [cuts in] You keep a respectful distance. You share
          a pint or a kebab. But there's an invisible line we
          don't cross.

Joanna   So you had no idea Peter was seeing this girl?

Roger   Course I didn't. The last conversation we had, of
          any length, was about gutter clearance.

Joanna   Did he sound as if he was going to be around to
          clear his gutters? In the long term?

Roger   You're asking me if I thought he was about to do

a runner? I've no idea. If Peter was in trouble and wanted to talk to me, he'd tell me directly and I'd listen ...

Joanna And then you'd slap him on the back and tell him to keep his chin up?

Roger There's far too much said about talking things over. Most things go away if you ignore them.

Joanna I'll stick that on your headstone.

Roger You're assuming I'll go first.

Joanna Statistically, you will.

Roger Exhausted by my wife's demands.

Joanna Do you want to be buried or cremated?

Roger [*saintly*] Whatever's easiest for you, dear.

Joanna I'll scatter your ashes beside the Pyramid Stage at Glastonbury.

Roger That'll muck up the sound system.

Joanna Of course, we might split up before you die.

Roger There is that to look forward to.

Joanna At least Sally hasn't got to worry about Peter's funeral now.

Roger I'm sure that'll be a great comfort.

Joanna Unless they get back together ... Is this affair serious? I wish you'd had a proper talk with him. Why didn't you take him for a coffee?

Roger I'd only just had a coffee with you. I didn't want another coffee.

Joanna You could have pretended you did. It's not much to ask. I'm sure Sally would have been grateful.

Roger Oh, so I was supposed to pump Peter for

	information about his new girlfriend and report back to Sally?
Joanna	Yes. She doesn't know what's going on.
Roger	She's not supposed to. He's left her.
Joanna	You are her link with Peter.
Roger	No I'm not. She's got her own link with Peter. She's got his mobile and his email. He's on Facebook if she wants to know anything.
Joanna	But he doesn't want to talk to her. He'd rather talk to you.
Roger	You're just making that up.
Joanna	You could help them get back together again. You could support him.
Roger	He doesn't need my support. He's got a new girlfriend who's a fitness instructor. She can support him. With one hand. She does push-ups.
Joanna	[*laughs*] You're jealous! Do you wish you were Peter?
Roger	Certainly not. He's losing his hair and he suffers from acid reflux.
Joanna	But he's got a new, young partner. Don't you wish you had?
Roger	I need the loo.

He gets up and goes to the downstairs cloakroom. Joanna raises her voice so he can hear her.

Joanna	You mean you need some thinking time!
Roger	I don't need to think!
Joanna	Have a look at the cold water tap while you're there. It's dripping!

Roger I don't do plumbing on an empty stomach.
Where's the soup?

Sound of distant humming.

Joanna You're humming again! Stop humming!

Sound of a text coming through for Joanna as Roger comes back.

Roger Who's texting?

Joanna My lover. He wants me to meet him by the
Co-op.

Roger Get some loo rolls while you're there.

Joanna Actually, it was Sally. Wondering if we'd heard
from Peter. I'll tell her you saw him this morning
but you didn't speak because you have a very
strange idea of the duties of friendship, shall I?

Roger Sure.

Joanna She'll be upset. That you missed an opportunity.

Roger What does she expect me to do? Trip him up?

Joanna You could have just strolled up and said 'hello'.
You talked to Sally, why didn't you talk to Peter?

Roger He was running.

Joanna For a bus?

Roger No. Running. In trainers and shorts. And a
headband.

Joanna laughs.

Joanna Peter! Running? In a headband? You didn't say he
was running.

Roger Well, I'm saying it now. He was running.

Joanna What did he look like?

Roger He looked like Peter. Running.

Joanna *She's* got him doing that. You should tell Sally that

	you saw Peter running. It would cheer her up, knowing he's not enjoying himself …
Roger	He looked perfectly happy.
Joanna	Red-faced and panting, wearing a rock band T-shirt, no doubt, with a heart monitor on his wrist. Did you tell her that?
Roger	No. Because it's not true. He looked quite cool and fit.
Joanna	That's annoying. She still loves him, you know. It's so sad, when friends split up, isn't it?
Roger	Sometimes. But now and then it's a really good idea.
Joanna	You mean like Steph and Terry?
Roger	Exactly.
Joanna	You remember that barbecue when Steph got completely hammered and gave him the ultimatum – 'It's me or the koi carp!'
Roger	He really loved those fish.
Joanna	You wouldn't do that, would you? Leave me for carp?
Roger	Never say never. They come in attractive colours.
Joanna	We know so many people that are splitting up. [*sighs*] Oh, it's been a horrible day, hasn't it?
Roger	That's because all we've done is maintenance.
Joanna	Maintenance?
Roger	Yes. Doc, dentist, optician.
Joanna	We used to be out all the time at parties, outings, suppers with friends.
Roger	Now we don't have invitations, just appointments.

Our social circle revolves around the physio and the practice nurse. I thought I might ask the physio to come to Istanbul with us. Be handy, with my knee …

Joanna blows her nose.

Joanna It's our fault.

Roger What is?

Joanna Sally and Peter's break-up. If we hadn't introduced them all those years ago, they wouldn't be splitting up now.

Roger That's technically true but somehow barking mad.

Joanna We had lots of lovely holidays with them, didn't we? Remember Tuscany? That rooftop dinner we had in Florence?

Roger When I got bitten by mosquitos?

Joanna And the South of France, when it did nothing but rain. But we laughed all the time …

Roger I don't remember laughing …

Joanna Especially when you fell off that boat.

Roger That was the start of my knee problems.

Joanna All those memories. All that history. It seems so stupid to throw that away for some gym instructor.

Roger Half his age.

Joanna You sound wistful.

Roger It's those new tablets. They make my throat dry.

Joanna No. I think you're wistful. Have you thought about having an affair?

Roger Of course I have.

Joanna	This is one of those moments when lying is the kinder option.
Roger	Everyone who's been married for more than five minutes has wondered what it would be like with someone else.
Joanna	Who else?
Roger	Just ... people you see on a train ... sometimes, someone you know.
Joanna	You mean friends? You fancy some of our friends?
Roger	Just a fleeting 'what if' thought ...
Joanna	Lusting after someone else?
Roger	Not lusting ... just daydreaming.
Joanna	When do you have these thoughts? All the time?
Roger	No. Just now and then. You know what I mean. When we're all sitting round having dinner with friends and the wine's flowing and ...
Joanna	And what?!
Roger	And some attractive woman laughs at my joke ...
Joanna	I've never seen that happen.
Roger	People exchange glances. You flirt with friends. You and Peter are quite flirty together.
Joanna	He's just like a brother. We get on well.
Roger	Yes, I know. So well, he put his hand on your thigh.
Joanna	When?
Roger	At Tony's sixtieth. You were sitting next to him on the sofa and ...
Joanna	He was helping himself up. That sofa was pretty low.
Roger	He could have used the chair arm.

Joanna You never mentioned that you noticed. Or that it bothered you.

Roger I didn't say it bothered me.

Joanna Well, it obviously did. If you're making such a big thing about it.

Roger I just said that I'd seen it happen.

Joanna Oh, I just wish Peter and Sally would get back together.

Roger Then you'd stop being jealous of me fancying her, would you?

Joanna Sounds like you're jealous of me and Peter.

Roger Sometimes I am and sometimes I think he's welcome to you.

Joanna You know what I said about honesty? Forget it!

Roger I think jealousy is quite healthy, providing it doesn't become homicidal.

Joanna And I think you'd like Peter and Sal to get back together as well.

Roger Then it must be true.

Joanna Do you think they will?

Roger Who knows?

Joanna I know we don't know, I'm just speculating.

Roger Well, I don't like speculating. They're our friends ...

Joanna He might be your friend but he's not my friend any more. He left Sally. And she's my friend. Or she was. Even though she's got a crush on you ...

Roger A crush? Where are we? The school playground? You can't cut off a friend just because he falls for someone else.

Joanna   Yes I can! How can you be friends with someone
who has done that?

Roger   You're completely inconsistent! You just said he
was like a brother to you and that I should talk to
him. Now suddenly I'm not supposed to be his
friend!

Joanna   I'm saying you can talk to him but make it
clear you don't approve and you're very …
disappointed in him.

Roger   Oh, please. I'm not disappointed. Well, I am
disappointed because we rely on his camper van
for Latitude but they've been married a long time.
Things change. People grow apart …

Joanna   Have we grown apart?

Roger   Right at this minute. Yes. Miles apart.

Joanna   An affair doesn't have to be a marriage breaker.

Roger   Maybe not, but it changes everything. Whether
you decide to stay together is up to you but it
will never be the same again, even if you say you
forgive each other. Now stop waving that ladle
around and give it to me. I'll do the soup.

Joanna   I'm sorry, I'm just feeling … a bit … low. The
dentist didn't help.

Roger   Why?

Joanna   Banging on about gum recession. 'You have to
expect it, at your age.' I don't expect *anything* to
be different! Why should I? I feel the same inside
as I did when I fell in love with Mick Jagger!
He's older than me but nobody tells the Stones

to stop doing what they've been doing all their lives!

Roger   Actually, quite a few people do.

Joanna It really is different for men. When I look in the mirror, I want to shout, 'OK, this is the outside but inside, I'm still dancing in the street with Martha and the Vandellas!'

Roger   Sounds like you're working yourself up to writing a feature. Good idea to write about getting older but feeling the same. And you've got quite a big birthday coming up; you could link it with that …

Joanna Yes, thank you! I know. And by the way, don't buy me a National Trust membership or a cardigan.

Roger   Thanks for the heads-up.

Joanna I want to go clubbing in Ibiza.

Roger   Not an ideal holiday, if I'm waiting for a knee replacement.

Joanna You don't have to come. Lots of couples have separate holidays.

Roger   Is this some perverse reaction to Peter and Sally splitting up?

Joanna What do you mean?

Roger   When friends split, it's supposed to bring you closer … grateful for what you've got. But not you. You want a single bed and separate holidays? Thanks very much!

Joanna I didn't say that. But there's a bit of you that's envious, isn't there? They're free again. Just to take off. Not to have to worry about … someone else.

Roger   With a dodgy knee?

Joanna Obviously, that restricts what we can do ... together.

Roger   [*hurt*] I didn't realise I was cramping your rampage round the nightspots of Europe.

Joanna I'm just talking about the things I've always done. Like dancing.

Roger   Clubbing, you said. When have you been clubbing in Ibiza?

Joanna Not Ibiza but Greece. After A levels. There weren't any clubs but a crowd of us went together – dancing on the sand, sleeping on the beach ... It was the Summer of Love.

Roger   And did Cliff Richard drive up in his double-decker bus, with Una Stubbs?

Joanna We never thought we'd have to worry about grey hair and reading glasses ...

Small pause.

Roger   Anyway, you're wrong. It's not different for men. We feel the same, too, and it hurts when some youngster pushes past and says, 'Scuse me, granddad!' A young woman was sitting on the train last week and she looked up at me and smiled and I smiled back and I had just a fleeting feeling of ...

Joanna Lust?

Roger   More like the warmth of a stranger liking the look of you. Then she put her hand on my arm ...

Joanna Oh?

31

Roger ... And said, 'Would you like my seat?'

Joanna Did you accept?

Roger No, I said thanks but I was getting off at the next stop. I wasn't but I had to leave the carriage because I was very close to crying.

Silence.

Roger Soup's ready.

Small silence again.

Joanna Thank you. For unblocking the sink.

Roger Is that a euphemism? And if so, for what?

Joanna No. I forgot to say at the time. I noticed you'd unblocked it and I'm very grateful.

Roger I also put the bins out.

Joanna Yes, but you always do that.

Roger So, no Brownie points for the bins but you like me because I've unblocked the sink?

Joanna Well, I thought we'd have to get the plumber in. That was a nasty blockage.

Roger It certainly was.

Joanna So thank you.

She gives him a kiss on the cheek.

Roger Woah!

Joanna It's just a kiss.

Roger It's never just a kiss. There's always a reason.

Joanna OK. When I saw you kiss Sally –

Roger *She* kissed *me.*

Joanna – I just thought it would be nice if we kissed each other, just for no reason. It's a nice habit to get into.

Roger A habit? You mean we'll have to do it all the time?

Joanna Why not? It's the first thing couples stop doing, after a long marriage. Kiss each other on the lips. And what it says in 'The Shoop Shoop Song' is so true. It *is* in his kiss!

Roger So Cher is your marriage counsellor, is she?

They laugh.

Joanna [*struck by a sudden thought*] We could wake up with a kiss as well. That would be nice.

Roger One step at a time.

Joanna Carol says she always knows when Ben wants sex because he cleans his teeth before coming to bed.

Roger Fascinating.

Joanna I always brush my teeth before I go to bed.

Roger I know. The soundtrack of my dreams is you gargling with the mouthwash as I drop off.

Joanna Which reminds me, you squeezed the tube in the middle again.

Roger Add it to my list of shortcomings.

Joanna [*persisting*] You don't always do it. Clean your teeth.

Roger I do. But not necessarily at the same time as you do.

Joanna You mean you do it secretly?

Roger You are so unsubtle. What you're saying is you've decided we should kiss each other goodnight and good morning but only if I've cleaned my teeth ...?

Joanna Yup. That's what I'm saying.

Roger Maybe I don't need to clean my teeth as much as you because I have perfect gums. Remember?

Joanna You can have perfect gums and stale breath ...

Roger You're not making me want to kiss you at the moment. Just saying.

Joanna I just think sometimes we could make more effort.

Roger Are you writing my school report?

Joanna I don't want us to drift on, ignoring each other ...

Roger I find it impossible to ignore you.

Joanna The first time we made love, you lit candles round the bed and put Dylan's 'Lay Lady Lay' on the stereo.

Roger I was trying to get you to have sex with me.

Joanna I'd have done that anyway. But I could see you'd taken such trouble. Everything looked very warm and inviting ...

Roger And the sheets were clean.

Joanna You read me Kerouac, in an American drawl ...

Roger 'With the coming of Dean Moriarty began the part of my life you could call my life on the road ...' Never fails.

Joanna What do you mean 'never fails'?!

Roger Are we having bread with this soup?

Joanna You don't do things like that any more.

Roger The first time you cooked me breakfast you were wearing a bikini with flowers in your hair ...

Joanna Isle of Wight Festival.

Roger You don't do things like that any more either.

Joanna I'm sad we're not [*treads carefully*] like that ... now.

Roger Show me any couple who've been married for forty years who are.

Joanna Steve and Emma. They haven't changed. They travelled the world in a Love Bus. And they were Rainbow Warriors for Greenpeace.

Roger And now he's on the Village Hall committee and they go on cruises. I'd say they've changed.

Joanna I mean romantically. They renewed their vows last summer.

Roger And you told me, 'What a nauseatingly tedious thing to do. We'll never do that.'

Joanna Maybe I was wrong.

Roger You're never wrong. You told me that as well. Now stop talking, sit down and eat your soup.

Joanna Thanks. That chair's got a wobbly leg.

Roger Tell me something I don't know.

Roger pulls out the chair. Joanna sighs.

Joanna I was quite happy when I woke up this morning but now I'm really fed up.

There's a crunch, as of someone sitting on a pair of new glasses.

Roger Well, here's something to cheer you up. I've just found your glasses.

END MUSIC
The Shoop Shoop Song – Cher

Just got this text from Sally. 'Gone to get my nails done, darling. Bertie won't be any trouble xxx Sal!' I'm still at the pool. Are you home yet? xx

I am. And guess what? Bertie's learned how to open the fridge! What a clever dog! We're now out of lamb chops. And he's ravaged the halloumi ...

This can't go on! Have you told him off? Put him in the garden!

Tried that. He's having lupins and geraniums for dessert. Going for a pint with Al

No! Stay there!

You'd better still be there when I get back ...

Or what?

I mean it!

Oooh ... Scared!

We Have No Secrets

OPENING MUSIC
Dream a Little Dream of Me – The Mamas & The Papas

SCENE 1: *The middle of the night. Joanna and Roger are in bed but Joanna has woken up.*

Joanna   So … you can't sleep either?

Roger   I can. I am asleep.

Joanna   I don't think so. I could hear your breathing change. It got faster.

Roger   That's because I was in the middle of a rather lovely dream. I'd like to go back to it, if you don't mind.

Joanna   Was it about Monica Bellucci again?

Roger   Might have been.

Joanna   You've fancied her ever since we saw her in *Spectre*. You were incandescent with rage. 'How could they sign her up for a Bond film and then only use her for about thirty seconds?'

Roger   I still feel the same. But I'm not sure if I was dreaming about her. I seem to remember a jumpsuit. So it could have been Anneka Rice.

Joanna   Why is it always three forty-two when you wake up in the night?

Roger   It isn't and I don't.

Joanna   Debbie says that the trick is to lie perfectly still. She says it's the tossing and turning that makes you more awake and if you lie like a knight on a tomb and stay completely quiet and don't move, you'll go back to sleep.

Roger   Could you try that, please? Now.

Joanna slides her arm across his body.

Roger   What are you doing?!

Joanna   Can't you guess?

Roger   Get off! We can't have sex! Sally's in the next room.

Joanna   So?

Roger   So … she'll hear!

Joanna   Sally's been 'in the next room' lots of times over the years, on holidays. We even shared a tent for a fortnight. It's never bothered you before.

Roger   That's because she was with Peter. They were a couple. It's fine when it's a couple but when someone's on their own, like Sally, it's upsetting to hear other people making love. It emphasises their loneliness.

Joanna   That's remarkably considerate of you.

Roger   I am considerate.

Joanna   Will you still be considerate in another month, maybe two?

Roger   What?! I thought she was just going to be here for a week!

Joanna She's here till Peter has finished tarting up the house.

Roger Well, that won't take long.

Joanna It will because Sally said he found out yesterday that he's got damp in the basement and he's doing it all himself and he's back and forth to Kirsty's now she's pregnant …

Roger Can't Sally go back and—

Joanna [cuts in] No! Sally can't go back and share the house with him!

Roger I was going to say can't she go back and hurry him up – or help him out?

Joanna She doesn't want to. How would you like to be in a house with someone you love, who doesn't love you?

Roger There are days when I am.

Joanna [laughs] Me too.

Roger Don't laugh. You'll wake Sally!

Joanna I think I have.

Roger What's that noise? Is she sobbing?

There is a sound of stuttering sobs.

Joanna Oh, poor Sally, crying herself to sleep … Do you think I should go and see if she's all right?

Roger No. Wait … wait … Listen!

More stuttering, whimpering sobs. Or is it? Joanna starts to get up.

Joanna I'll check on her.

Roger She's not sobbing. It's too regular. She's snoring!

They both listen.

Joanna   [*laughs*] Oh, crikey!

Roger   That's a surprise.

Joanna   Everybody snores sometimes.

Roger   Oh, believe me, I know. But I never heard her
          snore before.

Joanna   She's taken some sleeping tablets. It means she's
          probably in a very deep sleep. So …

Roger   So … A sudden noise would still wake her up.

Joanna   If she's going to be here a while, we're going to
          have to have silent sex.

Roger   That takes me back.

Joanna   To whenever we stayed with your parents …

Roger   Separate bedrooms!

Joanna   It was exciting, sneaking along the landing.

Roger   I had to go out and buy WD40. All the doors
          creaked and my mum had ears like a bat.

Joanna   Some of the best sex ever, though.

Roger   The chance of being caught out is a powerful
          aphrodisiac.

Joanna   I had the same feeling doing homework after
          school in my bedroom with my first boyfriend,
          Barry.

Roger   'Doing homework'. A classic euphemism.

Joanna   Sadly, no. My mum made me keep the bedroom
          door open.

Roger   A very successful contraceptive.

Joanna   We were almost faint with desire but nothing
          happened because I knew that any minute, Mum
          would come crashing through the door with a tea

tray and some Wagon Wheels and say, 'How's the homework going?'

Roger I climbed up a ladder once, to get into a girl's bedroom.

Joanna With a box of Milk Tray?

Roger No. We'd been doing *Romeo and Juliet*. She wasn't there and I discovered her window was painted shut. Then her dad's Ford Consul swung into the drive and stopped inches from the bottom of the ladder. He revved his engine. The ladder wobbled. I panicked and jumped off. And my knee's never been the same since.

Joanna Was it Sally? Who you were going to see?

Roger No! She'd moved away by then. And for the hundredth time, she was never my girlfriend. She just rugby tackled me in a game of kiss chase. And I wish I'd never mentioned it.

Joanna I'm just teasing you. There's something lovely about talking in the dark, don't you think? You can't see each other, so you can say anything.

Roger Like 'go to sleep'?

Joanna Is it really six months since Bonzo Dog died?

Roger Yes.

Joanna Do you miss having a dog?

Roger Yes.

Joanna Shall we get a rescue dog?

Roger Yes.

Joanna There are lots of cute puppies but so many beautiful older dogs who have been abandoned,

	or their owner has died and we could give one – or perhaps two – a lovely home, couldn't we?
Roger	Yes.
Joanna	And if you like a specific dog, like a Labrador or a husky, did you know each breed has its own rescue society?
Roger	Yes.
Joanna	I rather like the look of the Irish Red and White Setter. I've got a photo of one on my phone. I'll show you.
Roger	Look, I've said yes – and it's a collective 'yes' – to anything you've asked me. Enough. No more questions. And I know what an Irish Red and White Setter looks like, thank you very much. Goodnight.

Anguished cry breaks the silence.

Joanna	Oh, my God! What's that? What's happened to Sally?

Another anguished cry.

Roger	Hang on! That's not Sally. It's the bloody dog, howling!
Joanna	I thought she had Bertie in her room?
Roger	She said he'd be all right in his basket, in the kitchen. But clearly she was wrong. I'll go and let him out.
Joanna	Sally will hear him howling. She'll go.
Roger	I don't think so. I can still hear her snoring. Won't be a minute. You go to sleep.
Joanna	It's getting light. Hardly worth going to sleep now. Oh, listen, a blackbird.

42

Roger   Obviously female. No doubt her other half is still in the nest, with his wings over his ears …

MUSIC BREAK

Blackbird — The Beatles

SCENE 2: *Two hours later. The kitchen. The coffee is brewing.*
Roger is pouring a cup. Joanna enters, yawning.

Roger   Morning. So you *did* go back to sleep.

Joanna   [*yawns*] Amazingly, yes. How's the dog?

Roger   Confused but happy. I put down his breakfast but there's obviously a ritual, because he just kept staring at me.

Joanna   Sit. Wait. Eat. We tried it with Bonzo Dog, remember?

Roger   Unsuccessfully. Anyway, I just said, 'Bertie, I don't know what you're waiting for', so he shrugged and got stuck in. Coffee's on.

Joanna   Great. You could go back to bed, if you want to.

Roger   No thanks. Lovely day. Stuff to do.

Joanna   Like what?

Roger   Take the dog out. I've already cleaned the cars.

Joanna   Cars? Mine's in for a service …

Roger   I know. I've cleaned mine and … Sally's.

Joanna   You cleaned Sally's car?

Roger   Yes.

Joanna   Why?

Roger   Because it's under the tree and the rooks have

crapped all over it.

Joanna That was very nice of you –

Roger I am a nice person.

Joanna – but slightly creepy.

Roger Slightly *what*?!

Joanna Creepy. You know, like those guys who used to leap out at you at traffic lights and hose down your windscreen, even though you didn't want them to.

Roger Sally wasn't in the car. And I'm sure she'll be very happy it's clean.

Joanna I bet she will.

Roger Could you go out and come in again, in a better mood?

Joanna Well, she can clean her own car, like I do.

Roger When was the last time you cleaned a car?

Joanna I keep it immaculate.

Roger But you never go near a sponge and bucket. You get it valeted in the multi-storey car park.

Joanna *And* you spent an hour fixing the links on her bracelet yesterday!

Roger Yes, I did. It was very like your bracelet, I knew how to do it.

Joanna You're just being too nice.

Roger Well, that's a first. Too nice?

Joanna Yes. Smarmy nice.

Roger Look, Sally's our friend –

Joanna More your friend, I'd say.

Roger – and our guest. She's having a rough time and

44

I'm helping out, with things I can do for her.

Joanna She has to learn to do them herself, now she's on her own.

Roger Does she?

Joanna Yes, all the things Peter used to do for her, *she'll* have to do.

Roger So if I left, you'd be able to bleed the radiators, change the tyres and install patio doors, would you?

Joanna I can do all those things.

Roger You really are completely delusional. When have you ever changed a tyre?

Joanna I didn't say I had, I said I can. I know how to do it.

Roger Next time one bursts at night, in the rain on the M25, I'll just sit back and let you get on with it, shall I?

Joanna Easy peasy.

Roger You were the one who told me we had to step in and support Sally and look after her.

Joanna Yes, but I didn't say you had to be Parker to her Lady Penelope. 'Yus, m'lady. Clean your car, m'lady. Walk the dog ...' [*beat*] Oh, I'll be out tonight, by the way ...

Roger Good. Because I was about to throw you out.

Joanna I've got Pilates.

Roger Presumably Sally's going with you?

Joanna No, she's not.

Roger Why not?

Joanna   She said she just feels so wiped out, she hasn't got the energy. So, will you be all right? You and Sally? Together?

Roger   In what sense?

Joanna   Remember when we both gave up smoking? On the same day? At the same time?

Roger   To the minute. Twenty-eighth July nineteen eighty-six. Seven forty-five p.m. Which was extremely inconvenient, as Diana and Al were on their way round for a barbecue.

Joanna   I didn't want to stop, because I loved smoking and I enjoyed every one of my five Silk Cut a day. But you reached for a cigarette as soon as you opened your eyes in the morning and you had a hacking cough. You definitely needed to stop. So I gave up with you, because I knew you wouldn't do it on your own –

Roger   Because I have absolutely no willpower or self-control. And I'm a constant disappointment.

Joanna   – and we talked about how hard it was –

Roger   Yes. It was really tough.

Joanna   – and then, one day, I phoned you at work and Carl said, 'He's not here but he can't be far way because his cigarettes are on the desk.'

Roger   And you popped that into your 'never let him forget' folder and I suffered your seething wrath for the next ten years.

Joanna   No. You said, 'I promise we'll have no secrets, ever again.'

Roger   I did not!

Joanna   You did.

Roger   Well, if I did, I didn't mean it. It's a ridiculous promise to make. All couples have secrets. Carly Simon –

Joanna   Who you also fancy.

Roger   – wrote that song 'We have no secrets, we tell each other everything' as a joke, about a claustrophobic relationship.

Joanna   You couldn't give up smoking, could you?

Roger   Wherever you're going with this, I'm not coming with you.

Joanna   You have an addictive personality.

Roger   Ah. And you think I'm addicted to Sally?

Joanna   You like the fact that she's grateful and smiles at you.

Roger   Well, it's quite a novelty. But this is all rather insulting to both Sally and me. She's not a simpering airhead and I'm not Cyrano de Bergerac.

Joanna   But currently you're the only man in her life. So watch yourself!

Roger pretends to back off.

Roger   Ooh! Scared!

Joanna   Just treat her normally. Don't keep 'doing things' for her.

Roger   I'll have to make her some supper tonight.

Joanna   She's vegan.

Roger   I know that. I'll rustle up an Ottolenghi red rice and quinoa salad, shall I?

47

Joanna That might stoke the fires. Women like men who can cook.

Roger Sally likes to eat early …

Joanna [*clenched*] Does she?

Roger Yes, she said we often seem to eat a bit late for her.

Joanna Oh, really? I'll whack supper on the table at five from now on, shall I?

Roger Early is good because we can eat before the football starts. Sally likes football.

Joanna This is beginning to sound like a Ladybird book. *Sally has supper early, then Sally watches football. Happy Sally!*

Roger And I'm sure she won't eat much, so there'll be leftovers for you.

Joanna *Leftovers?!*

Roger Shush …

Joanna I won't shush!!

Roger I just heard the loo flush.

Joanna So what? I don't care.

Roger She's on her way down. I heard a creak.

Joanna That's her arthritic hip.

Roger Be nice.

Joanna Jeepers! Did you just run your fingers through your hair?

Roger I don't know. Did I?

Joanna Just stop acting like you want to be her *boyfriend*!

Door opens.

Roger Sally! Morning! I've given Bertie his breakfast and made some coffee.

Joanna And he's cleaned your car. Isn't he wonderful?

MUSIC BREAK
We Have No Secrets – Carly Simon

SCENE 3: *Later that morning. Joanna is heading out of the door with Bertie the dog. Roger is trimming the wisteria outside.*

Joanna	Come on! Quick! I don't want Sally to come with us.
Roger	What?
Joanna	We're taking Bertie out. Bertie! Walkies!
Roger	I don't want to.
Joanna	I want you to. Hurry up!
Roger	What's the panic?
Joanna	We need a good walk.
Roger	Do we?
Joanna	Yes and so does Bertie. Sally is so wiped out at the moment, he's not getting proper exercise and he's crapping all over the garden.
Roger	Are we just going round the block?
Joanna	No. Ten thousand steps a day. I've got my Fitbit. Keep up!
Roger	Could you just slow down a bit?
Joanna	There's no point in walking unless you stride out. You don't get the benefit when you amble. It's got to be a cardiovascular workout.
Roger	It hasn't *got* to be anything.
Joanna	Can you hold his lead a little firmer? And give him a jerk. He's peeing on every blade of grass.
Roger	Tell you what, why don't you take Bertie out and

49

	I'll just stay home and trim the wisteria?
Joanna	I want us to go out for a walk together.
Roger	Can't we just stay in together?
Joanna	No. Because it's a lovely day and we don't want to be stuck indoors. And also, Sally is always there.
Roger	Obviously. She's staying with us.
Joanna	Yes. But she's very apparent, don't you think?
Roger	Not especially, no.
Joanna	We can't do normal things while she's there.
Roger	What do you mean?
Joanna	We can't relax.
Roger	I'm quite relaxed.
Joanna	When somebody else is in the house, you don't behave normally.
Roger	I'm not aware that my behaviour has changed.
Joanna	That's because you're not sensitive to ambience.
Roger	Am I not? Well, that's another one to add to the list of My Failures.
Joanna	We can't have our usual conversations.
Roger	You mean arguments?
Joanna	I don't just mean that.
Roger	So what do you mean? I can't bend you over backwards on the kitchen table?
Joanna	We certainly can't be spontaneous. It's like we're on our best behaviour.
Roger	I didn't know you had a 'best behaviour'. I can't say I've ever seen any evidence …
Joanna	Are you comfortable with the way she appears at breakfast in that floaty kimono?

Silence.

Roger   Can't say I've noticed.

Joanna   Oh, stop it!

Roger   All right. I have noticed. But it's just what she wears to sleep in.

Joanna   Exactly. She gets out of bed and comes straight down, with almost nothing on and bed hair, and she thinks it's completely acceptable to sit down and tuck into the muesli and fruit, dressed – or rather, undressed – like that.

Roger   Isn't it?

Joanna   No! She should shower and put proper clothes on.

Roger laughs.

Joanna   Why is that funny?

Roger   I was just thinking of you at the Isle of Wight Festival. You certainly didn't have any proper clothes on.

Joanna   Yes, but we were young then. Now, we're all quite … mature.

Roger   She's in pretty good shape.

Joanna   Oh?

Roger   As you are. And you often wear floaty things.

Joanna   That's when it's just us two. But if I was staying with friends, I'd be hugely aware that I should shower and dress before breakfast. I think it's rather brazen.

Roger laughs again.

Roger   You sound like the Dowager Lady Grantham.

Joanna   I think you should say something to her.

Roger Me?!

Joanna She listens to you.

Roger So, if I say, 'Please don't wear floaty things at breakfast, Sally', she'll think it's because I'm inflamed by her underpinnings.

Joanna You could sound stern.

Roger She'd just laugh.

Joanna Should we let Bertie off here?

Roger Well, it's fenced in.

Joanna Off you go, Bertie! It's nice walking a dog again, isn't it?

Roger Pleasant enough, but I'm not sure why you dragged me out with you.

Joanna So we can talk. We can't talk when Sally's there all the time.

Roger What do you want to talk about?

Joanna Oh, hell. Did you bring the poo bags?

Roger No. Didn't even think about it.

Joanna He's having an enormous … Have you got a tissue or anything?

Roger Just walk away. Pretend he's not with us.

Joanna We can't do that! It's irresponsible.

Roger Stick and flick. That's what we did with Bonzo Dog. Here's a twig. Look away!

Joanna Did it work?

Roger Let's just say that if it was a golf swing, I'd be in the bunker.

Joanna Did you know Bertie peed on the sofa?

Roger Did he?

Joanna Sally laughed and said, 'Oh, he's just a bit insecure and he wanted to mark out his territory.' And she's had him on her bed the last few nights. On my 800-thread-count cotton sheets! She treats that dog like a baby. We never let Bonzo on the bed, did we?

Roger No, but he's her comforter at the moment. She needs him to cuddle.

Joanna And she's always talking to people on the phone late at night, keeping us awake.

Roger She doesn't keep me awake.

Joanna You'd sleep through a nuclear holocaust, but she has these rambling conversations in the middle of the night. God knows who she's talking to. And then there's the twenty minutes each morning when we have to be silent and creep about in our own house while she does her mindfulness. It's not very mindful if she doesn't notice how cheesed off we are! I think you should tell her to be more considerate.

Roger That's not going to happen. This won't last for ever, so just calm down … Where's Bertie?

Joanna I thought you were watching him!

Roger And I thought you were!

Joanna I can't see him. He's gone! What are we going to tell Sally?

Roger We're going to tell her he's bonked a retriever. Look! Over there.

Joanna Oh, thank goodness.

Roger   I don't think the owner would agree with you. He's coming over. I'll let you deal with this. See you at home!

Joanna   No. Sorry. I'm off to Pilates.

SCENE 4: *9 p.m. That night. Joanna opens the front door as Roger is coming down the stairs.*

Roger   Oh, hello! You're back early.

Joanna   No I'm not. Why are you wearing a bathrobe?

Roger   Because ... I've just had a bath.

Joanna   What for?

Roger   Why does anyone have a bath?

Joanna   You don't usually have a bath at night.

Roger   Well, I did tonight.

Joanna   Where's Sally?

Roger   Gone to bed.

Joanna   Really? It's only half past nine.

Roger   I know, but you were right. She's shattered. Almost fell asleep on my Ottolenghi.

Joanna   So did you have a bath *before* she went to bed?

Roger   Of course not! Stacked the dishwasher. Took Bertie out for a quick walk. Sally doesn't like going out in the dark.

Joanna   What?! Rubbish! She always jogs round the block before bedtime.

Roger   He's a strong dog, Bertie. It's like trying to hang on to the back of a truck.

Joanna   So did he pull you over in a puddle?

Roger   No. Why?

Joanna   Still struggling to work out why you needed a bath.

Roger   Well, my back was already a bit achy after washing the cars this morning and then moving the chest of drawers –

Joanna   What chest of drawers?

Roger   – so I thought a soaky bath would be a good idea.

Joanna   [*very deliberately*] What. Chest of drawers. Did you move?

Roger   The one in Sally's room.

Joanna   Why?

Roger   Because she asked me to.

Joanna   Why didn't she ask me?

Roger   She probably hadn't heard about your multiple handywoman skills and fell for the old cliché that heavy lifting is a man's job.

Joanna   It's not heavy.

Roger   I know, but Peter did everything for her and she's not capable like you.

Joanna   *Capable?!* How dare you!

Roger   You've never lost the ability to surprise me. What's wrong with capable?

Joanna   Who wants to be called capable?!

Roger   Capab … ility Brown?

Joanna   I want to be called sensuous, sparkling, captivating –

Roger   And you are *all* of those things and so much more.

Joanna   – I do *not* want to be called capable!

Roger   OK. Got it. Won't call you that again.

Joanna   So when did she ask you to move it?

Roger   After supper.

Joanna   Why did she want it moved?

Roger   She just said she'd like it under the window, so she could do her make-up in a better light.

Joanna   She could have put the mirror on the windowsill; there was no need to move the furniture.

Roger   She didn't move it. I did. It was no problem.

Joanna   No, it never is with Sally, is it? So, she invited you into her bedroom?

Roger   Strictly speaking, it's our bedroom. One of our bedrooms.

Joanna   What did she say, exactly?

Roger   She said, 'Can you come up and move my chest?'

Joanna   And didn't you think that was a bit funny?

Roger   In a *Carry On* sense, yes, I suppose it was.

Joanna   So was she wearing a bathrobe *as well*!

Roger   Neither of us were wearing a bathrobe.

Joanna   Oh?!

Roger   We were fully clothed. Talking over supper about getting used to the layout of unfamiliar rooms and how it's not easy sleeping in strange beds …

Joanna   She seems to be sleeping all right. Did you tell her we heard her snoring like a warthog?

Roger   What do you think?

He laughs.

Joanna   What's funny?

Roger   I quite like it that you're jealous.

Joanna   You think I'm jealous?

Roger   It's quite obvious. You're creating this soft-porn scenario of me leading Sally from the supper table, up the stairs, stripping down to my boxer shorts while she leans back on the pillows, trembling with desire, as I heave the chest of drawers single-handedly across the room, sweat pouring off my half-naked body. She beckons me and after some swift rumpy-pumpy we bathe together, soaping each other down, with that nice chestnutty bubble bath …

Joanna   Finished?

Roger   Just getting started.

Joanna   Clever trick. Laughing off what really happened as the imaginings of a crazed woman.

Roger   Talking of crazed, how was Pilates?

Joanna   David's back.

Roger   Your lentil-breathed groupie? I thought he'd left. Broken-hearted at your cool indifference.

Joanna   Apparently, he's been away on an assertiveness training course. He missed the first session because he didn't know which room it was in and didn't like to ask …

Roger   I believe you just made that up, for a laugh.

Joanna   If only.

Roger   Did he put his mat down behind yours again?

Joanna   'Fraid so. I thought of farting to put him off, because everyone farts in Pilates, but it seemed … a bit unkind.

Roger   Never stopped you before.

Joanna I could hear him breathing. Rather heavily. Behind me.

Roger Do you want me to have a word with him?

Joanna No! He gives me rhubarb from his allotment.

Roger But he might be dangerous.

Joanna He's not. He's a Buddhist and they get really upset if they accidentally tread on an ant and also he's physically very weak. I have to open his water bottle.

Roger That's because you're so capab—

Joanna [*cuts in*] Don't say it!

Roger So captivating and sensuous.

They both laugh.

Joanna Actually, I was quite tense, all through the class, because of David. I'm quite achy, too. I think I might do a hot-water bottle.

Roger Better idea. Why don't I run us a bath?

Joanna You've already had one bath today.

Roger Who's counting?

Joanna And what about Sally?

Roger Only room for two.

Joanna She'll hear us.

Roger I said a bath, not a bonk. Although ...

Joanna Well, it might be nice.

Roger Which?

Joanna Let's take up a glass of wine and find out.

Roger This the second time today I've followed a woman upstairs.

Joanna Don't spoil it.

Roger I'll bring the wine.

Joanna Oh, cripes! You've just had a bath!

Roger I think we established that.

Joanna There'll be no hot water left!

Roger We could switch on the immersion heater.

Joanna But don't you think by the time it heats up, the moment might have passed?

Roger I didn't know we were having a moment. I thought we were just having a wash.

Joanna [*laughs*] Give me a great big hug.

Roger What's the magic word?

Joanna Now! I'm sorry – and you're right.

Roger What? That's a sentence I only hear on my birthday. Is it my birthday?

Joanna I think Peter and Sally's break-up has affected us both more than we realise, don't you?

Roger Oh, let's forget about them and have an early night.

Joanna I've got that lovely body oil. You can give me a back massage.

Roger It'll make the sheets all mucky.

Joanna If we do it right …

They laugh as they walk upstairs.

MUSIC BREAK

Dream a Little Dream of Me – The Mamas & The Papas

SCENE 5: *Midday the next day. Joanna is sitting at the kitchen table. Roger comes in with some shopping. He puts the items down on the table.*

Roger   Why is it that when you buy more than three
             bottles of wine, they always ask you at the
             checkout, 'Having a party?'

Joanna   You've got two cases there, so it's a reasonable
             question.

Roger   I wanted to say, 'No. This'll just last us till Tuesday.'

Joanna   But what did you say?

Roger   I smiled wanly and said, 'How did you guess?'

Joanna   Pathetic. Did you show the store card?

Roger   Forgot.

Joanna   I'm going to put it on your keyring!

Roger   Fine. But here's the good news. I've got
             everything on the list, with no screw-ups or
             random substitutions. Cheese – mature cheddar.
             Mouthwash – no alcohol, mint flavour. Bacon –
             smoked streaky. And … bread.

Joanna   Soya and linseed bread?

Roger   Sally likes it.

Joanna   Well, Sally's not here.

Roger   Where's she gone?

Joanna   Her sister's.

Roger   I thought Elaine was in Italy?

Joanna   She came home yesterday.

Roger   OK. So, will Sally be back for lunch?

Joanna   No, she won't be back at all.

Roger   She's gone?

Joanna   She has. For good.

Roger   And … what? Moved in with Elaine?

Joanna   Yup.

Roger   What did you say to her?!

Joanna   I didn't say anything to her! It was her idea to go. She thought it was best.

Roger   Hey! [*he looks at her closely*] Have you been … crying?

Joanna   Not very much.

Roger   Well, something's upset you.

Joanna   Sally told me what really happened last night.

Roger   Ah. So you know about …?

Joanna   The kiss. Yes.

Roger   Right.

Joanna   Why didn't *you* tell me?

Roger   I didn't tell you because I didn't want to.

Joanna   We have no secrets …

Roger   Yes, we do! And this was one I wanted to keep.

Joanna   You DID keep it.

Roger   I had reasons for that …

Joanna   Sally and I had a long talk, after you went shopping. She came down with her bags packed, put Bertie on the lead and told me that you'd cooked her a wonderful meal and been so lovely and kind last night, and after you'd had few glasses of wine she'd helped you move the chest of drawers –

Roger   She didn't really help me very much …

Joanna   – and she dropped her end and you started singing 'Right, said Fred' and you were laughing and then …

Joanna gets tearful. Roger puts his arm around her.

Roger   Come on … Don't cry. It was nothing. Have this tissue … Bit crumpled.

Joanna It's OK. It's all right. She said that *she* kissed *you*.

Roger   I see.

Joanna And you didn't kiss her back.

Roger   She said that?

Joanna Yes, she said that. Is it true?

Roger   It is true. And that's the main reason why I didn't tell you about it, because I didn't want you to think badly of Sally and dump her as a friend, when it was obvious she was just desperately lonely and … needed some affirmation that she was still attractive.

Joanna But you didn't give it to her?

Roger   Not in any sense. No.

Joanna She said you stepped back … She was crying when she told me … You held her arms to her sides and said that you loved her as a friend but it would never be anything more. And that you and I had both had … flings, in the past and been on the verge of breaking up.

Roger   We did break up, on quite a regular basis.

Joanna Once, after you lied about not smoking! And she said that you told her you've realised, over the years, the terrible risk of losing everything if you play around, and now the possibility of ever losing me wakes you up at night in terror –

Roger   I had to exaggerate for effect.

Joanna – and seeing what happened to her and Peter

brought the fear back.

Roger   I told her what she needed to hear.

Joanna   You said that even if Monica Bellucci offered herself to you, you'd say 'no' because you don't love her. You love me.

Roger   I might have slightly over-stated the likelihood of my turning down a night with Monica Bellucci. Now, blow your nose, or I might change my mind.

Joanna   Sally said she felt so awkward and embarrassed and she started to cry in front of you and you gave her a box of tissues and a big hug and then made her a hot chocolate ... That's why you had a bath, isn't it?

Roger   I suppose I felt a bit weird and I was worried about you coming home. I told her I would never say anything to you, because ... you and Sally should stay friends.

Joanna   We will.

Roger   Good. Then my work here is done. I'll put the cheese in the fridge.

Joanna   You know what you are, don't you?

Roger   Oh, here we go. I thought I'd got off lightly.

Joanna   You're Chaucer's verray parfit, gentil knyght.

Roger   Thank you. But I'd rather be Monica Bellucci's arm candy.

END MUSIC

Don't Worry Baby – The Beach Boys

Do these by the time I get back from Pilates - or else! xxx Nurse Ratched.

PS! Do not go upstairs without me!

Can I go upstairs with Monica Belluccis?

LYING KICKS

Lie on your back with a 3-pound coffee can or rolled-up blanket under your involved knee.

Straighten that knee, hold for five seconds. Slowly lower your knee down and relax. Your knee should be in contact with the coffee can or blanket throughout.

Haven't got a 3-pound coffee can. Next!

HEEL SLIDES

3–5 minutes.

While in a sitting or lying-down position, loop a stretching strap over your foot and pull your knee into a bent position, as your foot slides towards your buttock. Hold a gentle stretch and repeat.

Tried this with a Samsonite luggage strap. Pinged in my face.

QUAD SET

2 sets of 10 repetitions. 5 second hold.

Tighten the top thigh muscles and attempt to press the back of your knee downwards.

I can do this one. But it makes my teeth ache

ISOMETRIC HIP ADDUCTION

2 sets of 10 repetitions.

Place a rolled-up towel between your knees and squeeze together, so that you squeeze the object firmly.

Reminds me of sex, in those early experimental days, darling!

BED MOBILITY EXERCISE

Lie on your back. Come up on both elbows. Straighten arms and come up into a sitting position. Lower back on to your elbows and lie down.

No! This is nasty. And completely unnatural. Who sits up like that? Apart from a chesty porn star ...

Lean on Me

OPENING MUSIC
Lean on Me – Bill Withers

SCENE 1: *Joanna and Roger have come home from the hospital after his knee operation. They are coming through the front door. Key in door. Front door crashes open.*

Joanna	OK. Now lean on me.
Roger	Right … right …
Joanna	Not that much!
Roger	Sorry.
Joanna	Just stop a minute. We've got to get through the door.
Roger	I know. I'm trying.
Joanna	Stop pushing!
Roger	I'm not pushing!
Joanna	Look, I will ease in sideways and then you can reach out your arm and hold on to me and … Not that arm!
Roger	Ooh, my knee! I just want to sit down.
Joanna	Well, you have to get through the bloody door first!
Roger	Everything hurts. My leg's not working … I feel a bit tearful. Coming home, at last …

Joanna You've only been away for one night. Where's the crutch?

Roger Dunno. I think I left it in the car.

Joanna Oh, useful. I'll go and get it.

Roger No! Don't leave me! I'll fall over! I don't need the crutch. I just need to hang on to you and get into the house and sit down.

Joanna Hold the door open, then.

Roger I can't!

Joanna Yes you can. And stop shuffling!

Roger I have to shuffle. I can't help it.

Joanna Old men shuffle.

Roger And very accomplished tap dancers.

Joanna I don't see you launching into a triple time step any time soon, do you?

Roger Ow! Double ow!

Joanna Chair's behind you.

Roger I can't feel it.

Joanna It's *there*!

Roger All right! You don't have to drag my arms back, unless you've got handcuffs.

Joanna I want you to feel the chair! Lower yourself down gently.

Roger Trying. Oooh! I can't bend my knee yet.

Joanna Oh, God! Right, well, I'll get behind you, under the arms and try to … You could help a bit!

Roger How?!

Joanna Hold on to the chair arms. Brace yourself.

Roger I've got no strength. I'm post operative, remember?

Joanna You have to help. Or I'll kick your legs from under you.

Roger Go away. I don't want you. I want the nice nurses from the hospital.

Joanna Tough bananas. I'm all you've got.

Roger When they asked me, 'Is there someone at home who'll look after you?', I said, 'Yes.' How wrong I was!

Joanna Stop talking and take some of the weight. I'm lowering you now. And … right. Don't move!

Roger Thank you, Matron.

Joanna I'm going to unload the car.

Roger Ermmm … actually. Before you do that, I think I might just need …

Joanna What?! What do you 'just need' *now*?!

Roger I'm afraid I have to go to … the loo. [*beat*] Ow! Was that a Chinese burn?

MUSIC BREAK
Ring My Bell — Anita Ward

SCENE 2: *Two hours later. The spare bedroom. Roger is shaking a toy cow with a ringing bell. He stops and then does it again. Joanna appears.*

Joanna What do you think you're doing?

Roger I found Bonzo Dog's cuddly cow. Now I can ring it whenever I want you.

Joanna throws it across the room.

Roger Don't do that to Buttercup!

Joanna And what *is* the emergency this time?

Roger I thought you could bring the small TV up here and I could watch the golf.

Joanna Did you?

Roger Why are you so cross?

Joanna This is the seventh time I've been up these stairs and you've only been home for two hours! What did the doctor say to you?

Roger He said I was in pretty good shape for a man of my age. Everything was looking tip-top and—

Joanna [*cuts in*] He said you're not an invalid. You've just got a new knee. Your successful rehabilitation depends on your commitment to follow the home exercise programme.

Roger He also said I would feel tired and should rest in the day.

Joanna Well, you've certainly rested. Where's that piece of paper?

Roger Which one?

Joanna The exercise sheet.

Roger I thought you picked it up.

Joanna It better be with these notes, or … right. Here it is. Number One. Stretch out your leg and lift it …

Roger makes a feeble attempt.

Roger I've only just come home. Can't we start tomorrow?

Joanna No. This is the easy bit. You have to do this before you get out of bed every morning. Up and down. Up and down … Tomorrow, we're going up the

stairs and— Don't stop doing the lifts! You need
to do at least ten. And then we'll do the ankle
pumps and the lying kicks.

Roger   Good name for a band. The Lying Kicks!

Joanna   We need a rolled-up towel for that.

Roger   The fun never ends, does it?

Joanna   Concentrate!

Roger   It's not easy to balance on a single bed. I don't see
why I can't be in our bedroom.

Joanna   Because you need a pillow under your knee. And
you'll be sighing and whimpering all night.

Roger   No I won't. I've got painkillers.

Joanna   Are you sure?

Roger   Yes, they're here. Within reach. But I might just
need you to bring me a little …

Joanna   What *now*?

Roger   [*warily*] A little more water?

Joanna   [*heavy sigh*] Why didn't you ask me for water
when I brought up the paper?

Roger   Because you slapped the paper down and left,
faster than a speeding whippet, without even
resting a cool hand on my fevered forehead.

Joanna   It's not fevered, and I do have other things to do
apart from waiting on you all day.

Roger   I'm so glad I didn't marry you just for your
bedside manner.

Joanna   So. Now you want *water*!

Roger   No matter. I'll swallow them dry and probably
choke to death …

Joanna I'll get you some water. OK?

Roger [*doing his best Jack Nicholson in* One Flew Over the Cuckoo's Nest] I'm sure sorry, ma'am, Gawd but I am.

Joanna You are not Jack Nicholson and I'm certainly not Nurse Ratched!

Roger No, you're not Nurse Ratched.

Joanna Thank you.

Roger You're much more like … Remember that film – *Misery* – with Kathy Burke …?

Joanna Bates. Kathy Bates.

Roger Where she kept Clint Eastwood prisoner?

Joanna James Caan.

Roger No, I don't think so.

Joanna Yes, it was James Caan.

Roger Anyway, she kept him a prisoner and tortured him …

Joanna I'm not keeping you a prisoner. Far from it. I want you to stop malingering.

Roger Proper nurses don't say things like that.

Joanna They would after five minutes with you. Get up!

Joanna whips the duvet off.

Roger Give me my duvet back! I'm cold! And I want Buttercup!

Joanna She's in the bin. Now, get dressed.

Roger Maybe if you wore an upside-down watch and a starched apron, you'd discover your inner Florence Nightingale.

Joanna She didn't stand any nonsense either. On your feet.

Roger I'd like a little privacy, please. Screens, Nurse!

MUSIC BREAK
Ring My Bell – Anita Ward

SCENE 3: *Joanna and Roger's bedroom, late that night. Joanna is asleep in bed. Roger enters, shuffling, tapping a crutch. He's stumbling about, banging his knee and opening drawers, muttering and yelping. He bangs his knee again.*

Roger   Arghhhh! Stupid place to put a bedside cabinet!
Joanna wakes up, cross.
Joanna   What the hell are you doing?!
Roger   I need my tablets.
Joanna   You said you had painkillers by the bed!
Roger   Not the painkillers. I've got indigestion. Probably all the stress.
Joanna   Maybe you're having a heart attack.
Roger   Do you think so?
Joanna   No, I don't. You shouldn't be in here, rummaging. You could fall over.
Roger   I wouldn't have to rummage if I could put the light on!
Joanna   You're shuffling again. Stop shuffling!
Roger   I have to shuffle. I can't see where I'm going.
Joanna   You can feel for your tablets.
Sound of foil rustling.
Joanna   There. You've got them. I can hear them rustling.
Roger   They might be the wrong ones.
Joanna   Let's assume not. Goodnight.
Roger   What would happen if I took the anti-

inflammatories, when what I need is indigestion relief?

Joanna Nothing. They probably contain similar stuff.

Roger This doesn't feel like a red box.

Joanna What does 'red' feel like?

Roger Maybe the Rennies are on your side …

Joanna Get off me!

Roger I'm trying, but my knee seems to have … Ow! … Locked.

Joanna [*heavy sigh*] Dear Lord!

She switches the light on.

Joanna Satisfied?

Roger Argh! You might have warned me!

Joanna Can you see a red box now?

Roger No. I can't see anything. I'm blinded.

Joanna Here it is!

She throws it at him.

Roger Don't throw it! Now I really have hurt my knee. Argh.

He whimpers.

Joanna I'm going to have to ask you to leave quietly.

Roger I would if I could but my knee has given up supporting me and I am prostrate, at your mercy.

Joanna Maybe I'll whack your other knee with the hairbrush, that should get you going.

Roger Lawks, Miss Discipline. I know people pay good money to be treated like this but I just want a little TLC and it's my bedroom as well, you know.

Joanna Not tonight it isn't.

Roger   I'd crawl out of the door if I could put weight on this knee. Anything to make you happy. But I can't move … Owww!

Joanna sighs.

Joanna   Oh, for goodness' sake. All right. I'm going to pull you back up the bed.

Shuffling and 'Ow's.

Roger   Thank you. That's much better. Can you straighten my pyjamas, Sister?

Joanna   I'm not indulging your nurses and patients fantasy.

Roger   I thought you'd find it exciting. My hot breath on your neck as you heave me on to the bedpan.

Joanna   You're wheezing and, oddly enough, the clank of your crutch didn't sound like the overture to a night of passion.

Roger   Good job this isn't our first date, isn't it?

Joanna   I don't think you realise how scary it was – waking up to find you looming over me.

Roger   You used to love it.

Joanna   That was when you had all your parts in working order.

They both laugh.

Joanna   But I'm really cross with you. You could have done some serious damage to your knee.

Roger   You said I had to walk about.

Joanna   Not in the middle of the night!

Roger   I'll just lie here quietly, then. You won't even notice me.

Joanna   Go to sleep.

Roger   I can't sleep until the agonising pain in my knee subsides.

Joanna   Well, I'm going to sleep.

Roger   Oh, before you do that, could you just …?

Joanna   I've straightened your pyjamas and your pillows. What else?!

Roger   Could you … possibly … help me to the loo again?

MUSIC BREAK
Lean on Me – Bill Withers

SCENE 4: *The next morning. They are at the kitchen table. Roger is reading the paper. Joanna is trying to get him to exercise.*

Roger   Any more coffee left?

Joanna   No. Because we're about to go start doing the exerci—

Roger   [*cuts in*] What is wrong with this sentence: 'Zookeepers have adopted a baby wallaby and it is being weaned from four-hourly feeds by its adopted parents.'

Joanna   There's nothing wrong with it. It's a lovely story.

Roger   Obviously, it should be adop*tive* parents, not adop*ted*.

Joanna   Should it?

Roger   Of course! The wallaby was adopted – by adoptive parents. They are not his adopted parents.

Joanna   How do you know it's a he?

Roger   It doesn't matter what sex he is! *It* is. The point is it's grammatically rubbish. He didn't adopt them.

Joanna   He might have. He might be a pushy wallaby.

Roger   Ye gods!

Joanna   Perhaps he hopped up to them and said, 'Oy, cobber! I want you to be my mum and dad!' Then they'd be his adopted parents, wouldn't they? Cos it was his idea. It's dangerous jumping to conclusions. We may not know the whole story. Now, it's time we carried on with your—

Roger   [*cuts in again*] Good grief! Trafalgar Square lions could give you conjunctivitis! Listen to this! Experts swabbed twenty-four famous statues and found high levels of bacteria. They advise washing your hands after rubbing a monument. Can you believe that?

Joanna   I know what you're doing.

Roger   I'm reading the paper.

Joanna   You've been reading it for over an hour.

Roger   There's a lot of news.

Joanna   Wallabies and statues? You're just putting it off.

Roger   Putting what off?!

Joanna   Exercises. Come on. Stairs today.

Roger   But I haven't even got to the sports pages!

Joanna   Tottenham won. Manchester City lost. Move!

Roger   I'm trying.

Joanna   Mind the chair. Walk this way.

Roger   If I walked that way, I wouldn't need a knee operation. Boom-tish! I thank you!

They reach the bottom of the stairs.

Joanna Hold on to the banister.

Roger Oh, I intend to.

Joanna Now, lead with your good leg.

Roger I don't have a good leg. They're both useless.

Joanna The good leg is *not* the one that has a new knee.
That is the bad leg. God, I sound like a *Blue
Peter* presenter. So. Put your good leg – and your
weight – on the first step. Lean slightly forward
and then lift up your bad leg to join it.

Roger Can't.

Joanna Yes you can.

Roger It hurts.

Joanna Obviously there will be twinges, but be a brave
little soldier.

Roger [*sulking*] Don't want to.

Joanna In that case, stuff it, I'm going to Pilates.

Roger Don't go! Sorry. I'm trying. Look … Good leg, ba
– ow, ow – ad leg …

Joanna And again. Good leg first, bad leg next.

Roger Oh, that wasn't as hard as I thought. Shall we have
a coffee?

Joanna You've only done two steps. Another twenty to
go. Come on.

Roger I've remembered.

Joanna What?

Roger Rosa Klebb. That's who you remind me of.
Although, I think even she had a flicker of
compassion.

Joanna Stop talking and keep walking. Good leg, bad leg. Good leg ... Sounds like ballet classes, when we pointed our toes and then flexed them. 'Good toes, naughty toes! Good toes, naughty toes!'

Roger This is really tough.

Joanna No gain without pain.

Roger If I was interviewing you for a job as my physio, you wouldn't get it.

Joanna I wouldn't want it.

Roger Or even my carer. I'd ask for someone else.

Joanna I'm not a carer.

Roger That's apparent.

Joanna Although, I suppose one day I might be, as bits of you are obviously falling off. No, not the bad leg first! Start again.

Roger I need to sit down.

Joanna Well, sit on the stairs for five minutes and then you can carry on.

Roger Come and sit with me.

Joanna I don't want to.

Roger Please. I'd put my arm around you but I might fall over.

Joanna Just get up the next two steps to the landing then.
Roger continues, with heavy breathing and sighs.

Roger OK. Nice leg, rubbish leg ... super leg, gimpy leg ...

Joanna That's it. Careful. Hold on to the banister. Ease down slowly. And ... sit.

Roger Yeeowch! The pain! The agony!

Joanna You realise you'll beep every time you go through airport security now. You'll get taken aside and patted down and hold everyone up.

Roger Any chance of the bright side being looked on?

Joanna And you have to get a letter from the doctor to say you've got lumps of metal in your body.

Roger I'm guessing Iron Man has the same problem.

Joanna We'll have to allow extra time at check-in.

Roger [*sighs*] It's the beginning of the end, isn't it?

No answer from Joanna.

Roger Say something.

Joanna Yes, probably.

Roger Say something *else*!

Joanna Well, it's a glimpse of what might happen in the future. One or other of us is bound to get less able, more dependent on the other.

Roger But it's unlikely to be you, is it? Honed with Pilates and forty lengths of front crawl three times a week?

Joanna True. But I'll always be there for you.

Roger I don't want your pity.

Joanna And you haven't got it.

Roger I'm just a gimpy wazzock, aren't I?

He sighs.

Joanna Yes. But you're my gimpy wazzock and I'm going to get you back to full mobility if it's the last thing you do.

Roger You mean 'If it's the last thing *I* do'.

Joanna I know what I mean.

MUSIC BREAK
Bend Me, Shape Me – Amen Corner

SCENE 5: *Two weeks later, outside the doctor's surgery. Joanna is in the car and Roger has just opened the passenger door to get in.*

Joanna Quick! Hop in!

Roger Is that likely to happen?

Joanna Move it! I've just seen the traffic warden.

Roger I'm sure he wouldn't give you a ticket, when he can see you're assisting an invalid ...

Joanna revs the engine and starts to move.

Joanna I have a history with him. He tried to move me on last week!

Roger Then he's a dead man walking. Woah! Slow down! You can't take off like that! My leg's hanging out.

Joanna Well, get it in!

Roger Promise me you'll never volunteer to drive hospital patients.

Joanna So what did the doctor say?

Roger He said the knee was a bit swollen and I'd been overdoing the exercise.

Joanna Don't believe you.

Roger Come back and ask him, then! You think I'm making it up?

Joanna Are you?

Roger No. He said exercise is good but in moderation. I must also rest.

Joanna   That's all you've been doing! Did he say how much longer this would go on?

Roger   Everybody's different, he said. But he thinks I'm doing remarkably well.

Joanna   Really?

Roger   Yes, really!

Joanna   OK. Surprised, that's all. So did you ask him if we can go to France at the weekend?

Roger   It's obvious we can't go to France, when I can't drive and I can't walk properly.

Joanna   But it's Millie's birthday party!

Roger   I know. I'm sorry. What else can I say?

Joanna   You could say, 'You go, darling, and I'll stay at home. I'll be fine.'

Silence.

Joanna   Well?

Roger   But I wouldn't be fine left alone. I might fall. And then …

Joanna gives him an exasperated look.

Roger   *What?*

Joanna   I'll get you one of those beepers you can put round your neck. Someone will come and heave you into an ambulance.

Roger   But not you. You'll be sashaying along the Croisette in Cannes.

Joanna   No, of course I won't. I'm not really going without you. But it's been two weeks and I'm just thinking aloud, in case this goes on for much longer …

Roger   I was reading some leaflets in the doctor's. About planning for future needs …

Joanna   Don't tell me. You want a stairlift and handles on the bath.

Roger   Not yet, but we have to face it. We're not going to live for ever.

Joanna   I am.

Roger   And we have no children to look after us. And I've got the beginnings of cataracts and my blood pressure's damn well up again and he wants me to have a test for diabetes …

Joanna   Hey! What's the matter? You're not …? Hang on, let me just pull over.

A car sounds its horn behind her. She turns round to shout at it.

Joanna   Yes! I am stopping here, because my husband's crying, you pork-faced butcher!

Roger   What kind of insult was that?

Joanna   Never mind him. Why are you so upset, darling?

Roger   It's just … Oh, I hate that my body's letting me down and I can't keep up with you.

Joanna   Well, you never could.

Roger   I can't even keep up with my friends. Peter's training for the Marathon.

Joanna   He's doing that to impress Kirsty. Sally said the only time she saw him run in thirty years of marriage was to get to the pub before closing.

Roger   [*quietly, looking out of the window*] The doctor asked if I was depressed and I thought maybe I am.

Joanna   Most people feel low after an operation.

Roger	What if I never get fully mobile again?
Joanna	[*briskly*] I'll leave you, obviously.
Roger	Where would you go?
Joanna	I have my running away fund.
Roger	What? Your *what?*
Joanna	You remember. My dad opened an account for me, before we got married.
Roger	Oh, that. Your deposit account.
Joanna	We called it my running away fund.
Roger	Who's 'we'?
Joanna	Dad and me.
Roger	Why did you call it that? Oh, let me guess …
Joanna	He was just worried that …
Roger	You'd married the wrong man?
Joanna	You know he liked you.
Roger	But he would have preferred it if I'd been in the RAF.
Joanna	No one was going to be good enough for his daughter.
Roger	What hurt most was when he made me stand on the edge of my own wedding photos and said, 'When you two split up, we can cut you off.'
Joanna	It was a joke.
Roger	Like the running away fund?
Joanna	It's been useful. There were times when I had to dip into it.
Roger	Countless times. Can't be much left.
Joanna	Actually, there is a tidy sum.

Roger   How much?

Joanna   It's mine! You don't need to know.

Roger   I do, if I'm getting my affairs in order.

Joanna   Stop talking like that!

She wipes away a tear.

Roger   Oh, don't you start crying!

Joanna   I hate seeing you like this. It's so unlike you.

Roger   I don't feel like me any more. I can't trust my body to do what I want. I hate it.

Joanna   But even when you're not firing on all cylinders, I still fancy you rotten, if it's any consolation.

Roger   It is. Thank you.

Joanna   Did you ask the doctor when we could have sex again?

Roger   Says my one-track-mind wife …

Joanna   I'm just thinking of things to make you feel better. Well, did you?

Roger   Of course not! We're both Englishmen. I didn't want to embarrass him.

Joanna   He's a doctor. It's his job to be asked embarrassing questions and not laugh out loud.

Roger   My thoughts are that we'll take it slowly. Might be a bit stop and start. I can't kneel for a while, so you'll have to go on top. Or we could try sideways. And I'll probably get cramp …

Joanna   If this is your seduction technique it needs work.

SCENE 6: *The next morning. Their bedroom. Roger is asleep.*
Joanna comes in with a cup of tea.

Joanna Good morning, darling.

Roger Bloomin 'eck!

Joanna I've come to wake you with a big kiss [*kiss*] and a lovely cup of tea.

Roger What time is it?

Joanna The sun is up and it's a beautiful day and I very much hope you're feeling better.

Roger Who are you? What have you done with my wife?

Joanna I thought we might go out for a little stroll today.

Roger Did you?

Joanna But only if you're really, really happy with the idea. Now, shall I give you a little massage on your poor, sorely legs?

Roger Actually, forget the wife, I'll keep you instead.

Joanna Look, I know I've been a bit tetchy lately.

Roger You've been an absolute cow.

Joanna But it's only because I hate to see you struggling and I'm worried about you and sometimes that means I snap.

Roger Like a menopausal crocodile.

Joanna I deserve whatever you throw at me but I'm determined to be nice from now on, because I love you.

Roger That's very kind. Disconcertingly kind.

Joanna I'm now going to run you a bath.

Roger   I don't want a bath.

Joanna   Why not?

Roger   I just don't. Not at the moment.

Joanna   Right. No matter. Look, I've been out and bought you some lovely croissants for breakfast …

Roger   I don't fancy a croissant. I'd prefer a bacon sandwich.

Joanna   Not a problem. And I've got you some flowers. Smell them.

Roger   No thanks. They make me sneeze.

Joanna   OK. I'll take them downstairs. Shall I help you get dressed?

Roger   I think I can do it myself. In fact, I should do it myself.

Joanna   [*sigh*] I'm not sure you can, but I've ironed the denim shirt and pressed your navy-blue cords. Did all that before you woke up, so it would be all ready for my darling husband …

Roger   I'd rather have a T-shirt, and the cords are too rigid. I need something loose.

Joanna   Do you indeed?

Roger   Yes, I do. Get me those linen summer trousers.

Joanna   What?!

Roger   Get me those—

Joanna   [*cuts in*] I heard you. Get them yourself!

Roger   Ah! My wife is back in the room. Normal service is resumed.

Joanna   Shuddup.

SCENE 7: *A few days later. Roger is sitting at the kitchen table. Joanna has been out and comes back into the house, calling out.*

Joanna   Hi, honey, I'm home!

Roger   Missed you. Love you to the Co-op and back!

Joanna   That reminds me. Forgot the dishwasher tablets …

She enters the kitchen.

Roger   Your hair looks nice.

Joanna   I've had my legs waxed.

Roger   I know. Just continuing the light banter.

Joanna   Have you been OK?

Roger   Absolutely fine.

Joanna   Not quite *fine* enough to empty the dishwasher.

Roger   You have to bend. I can't bend yet. I'm not allowed to.

Joanna   You've had visitors, then?

Roger   What?

Joanna   Visitors.

Roger   What do you mean?

Joanna   How else can I put it? People who come into the house who don't live here?

Roger   Oh, visitors.

Joanna   Yes, them. Who was it?

Roger   Meant to say …

Joanna   Really?

Roger   You didn't give me a chance. Peter called round.

Joanna   Did he?

Roger   Yes. To see how I was.

Joanna   *And?*

87

Roger   *And* I told him I was doing fine, thanks to my compassionate carer.

Joanna   *And* … Who else?

Roger   Did I say there was anybody else?

Joanna   No, you didn't. That's why I'm asking.

Roger   Why do you think somebody else came?

Joanna   Because there are three dirty mugs in the sink.

Roger   No shit, Sherlock.

Joanna   So? Who was it?

Roger   Not telling you.

Joanna   Oh, come on! I'm hoping it wasn't …

Roger   Yes, it was Kirsty. And she brought the baby.

Joanna   While I wasn't here?

Roger   Would you have wanted to be here?

Joanna   So are you saying they just dropped in while they were passing?

Roger   I could say that but you wouldn't believe me.

Joanna   Were they hiding round the corner, until they saw me drive away?

Roger   No, but Peter knows you're not keen on either of them and that you don't want to see him. But he cares about both of us – obviously, mostly about me at the moment, because, I'm … y'know …

Joanna   Sneaky.

Roger   Incapacitated. Peter just texted and asked when would be a good time.

Joanna   And you said when I'm not around?

Roger   No, I didn't. But I did say you were going to be out this morning.

Joanna   And he immediately said 'I'll come then'?

Roger   Yes, he did. But it wasn't a secret.

Joanna   No? [*she spots the open biscuit tin*] Hey! Did you
         give them those astronomically expensive Belgian
         chocolate biscuits?

Roger   I offered but Kirsty is still eating very healthily, as
         she's breastfeeding.

Joanna   Of course she is.

Roger decides to distract Joanna with helpful information.

Roger   She ate lots of leafy greens, oily fish, whole grains
         and fresh vegetables when she was pregnant, she
         said. And obviously, no alcohol.

Joanna   What are you, her nutritionist?

Roger   And that's why he was such a big healthy baby.
         She didn't need an epidural!

Joanna   You sound as if you have the faintest idea what
         that means.

Roger   She's got her figure back …

Joanna   You noticed?

Roger   She told me.

Joanna   Right. I think I'll go and watch paint dry.

Roger   What's the matter with you?

Joanna   I think 'not interested' will do, for starters.

Roger   I took a photo of him.

Joanna   Why?

Roger   Why not? Doesn't everyone take pictures of
         babies? *And* …

Joanna   Oh. Another '*and*'.

Roger   OK. *And* Peter's asked me to be godfather.

Joanna That's ridiculous.

Roger Why? I'm already a godfather to three—

Joanna [*cuts in*] Five.

Roger Five. And I'm good at birthdays and outings.

Joanna The last time you were asked to be a godfather was John and Liz's twins.

Roger Yeah, we had one each, didn't we? I had … ermmm …

Joanna Theo.

Roger Of course. And you're godmother to Sophie …

Joanna And they were twenty-eight last month.

Roger Are you saying I'm too old to be a godfather?

Joanna Of course you are! You're supposed to be a guardian if anything happens to the parents. But you'll probably be dribbling in a bath chair by the time he goes to big school.

Roger I did suggest they choose someone younger and they said they have. Kirsty's brother and Peter's nephew. But they want me as a kind of honorary godfather.

Joanna What does that mean?

Roger What does *any* honorary award mean?

Joanna It means you've been around for years but don't deserve a proper prize.

Roger I was rather touched.

Joanna So you said 'yes'?

Roger I did.

Joanna Without talking to me?

Roger You weren't here!

Joanna   [*darkly*] You made sure of that.

Roger   Look, they both asked how you are –

Joanna   I bet you said 'still seething'.

Roger   – and of course, they want you to be part of this.
          Actually, Peter wondered if I thought it was a
          good idea to ask you as well.

Joanna   As well as what?

Roger   As well as *me*, to be godparent to the baby. Which
          I thought was generous.

Joanna   Generous?!

Roger   Yes. You don't really deserve it. You've dumped
          them as friends.

Joanna   I've dumped him as a friend, because he left my –
          our – very good friend, Sally.

Roger   You can't seethe for ever.

Joanna   You've seen how upset Sally's been, especially over
          the baby.

Roger   But we've got lots of friends who have split up –
          and mostly, we've become friends with their new
          partners.

Joanna   Peter and Sally are different. *Were* different. We were
          all so close. It's like us breaking up. It's a big thing.
          I can't start being matey with the person who split
          them up. I don't even know her. Why would I want
          to be godmother to her squealing brat?

Roger   Actually, Hermes was rather smiley.

Joanna   Who?

Roger   He's called after the Greek God of athletes. Fast
          mover. Cos Kirsty's a fitness trainer.

Joanna That's no excuse. Hermes? Poor kid. He'll need to be a good runner. There'll be kids chasing after him, calling him [*she casts about for inspiration*] Germy!

Roger I think he'll be big enough to take care of himself. Look at the picture.

Silence.

Roger Well?

Joanna All I can see is a photo of your foot.

Roger What?! Oh, no! We'll just have to have them round again.

SCENE 8: *A few days later. Roger's up in the study. Joanna appears.*

Joanna Oh, there you are. I'm impressed you made it up three flights!

Roger Took me half an hour. I'm ready for a nap.

Joanna Me too. I've been trying to tidy the garden.

Roger I'm sorry. It'll be a while before I can help with that.

Joanna Why don't we get a gardener in?

Silence.

Joanna What do you think?

Roger Just one more thing I can't do any more.

Joanna Oh, good grief, stop moaning.

Roger First, the knee, then, no doubt, the hip …

Joanna No, I think the other knee will go first.

Roger So much to look forward to!

Joanna Look, Arnold Schwarzenegger was only fifty-five

when he had a hip replacement and Lionel
Richie was just sixty-one. Didn't stop them.

Roger How do you know this?

Joanna I was reading up on orthopaedics, cos I know
you're fed up but actually you're doing pretty well
for your age.

Roger God, that's patronising.

Joanna I can't say a thing, can I?! Be nice! You're lucky to
have someone here for you.

Roger Who trained at the Hattie Jacques school of
patient care.

Joanna Right. That's it. I'm going to Waitrose.

Roger I'm sorry. I just can't stop thinking about our
'future needs'. I don't want to be the old couple
who stay in their big house but can't get up the
stairs so they make a bedroom up in the dining
room. I think we should buy a bungalow. Now.
Before we have to.

Joanna What?! No, that's giving in. Walking up and
down stairs is the best exercise. If you move to a
bungalow, you'll certainly lose the use of your legs
much quicker.

Roger I just can't imagine a time when I can go upstairs
with ease again.

Joanna Why don't we get you a static bike? That will
strengthen your knee. And a Lycra bodysuit.

Roger Ye gods!

Joanna It'll cheer you up.

Roger It won't.

Joanna It'll certainly cheer me up! Look, there are millions of people in the world much worse off than you.

Roger That doesn't help at all. I've been looking at retirement home websites …

Joanna You can forget that.

Roger OK, well, how about buying a big house with our friends and living together, looking after each other? We've talked about it. We could call it the House of the Setting Sun.

Joanna I think *The Best Exotic Marigold Hotel* has a lot to answer for. After seeing that, hundreds of couples sold up and moved into a big house with friends and now they want to kill each other.

Roger Sally and Peter were up for it, remember?

Joanna Not any more. And we could never agree on who else we'd ask.

Roger Diana and Al would be good. She's a nurse. Useful.

Joanna But he's a control freak and I don't like his snorty laugh.

Roger Simon and Katrina?

Joanna She plays the violin and they've got a parrot.

Roger Jacky and—

Joanna [*cuts in*] No!

Roger But George is a carpenter.

Joanna And Jacky is a pain in the neck. Always quoting the *Daily Mail*.

Roger I just thought it would be good for you to have company, if I start to be a burden.

Joanna Too late. So. Apart from wallowing in self-pity, what are you doing up here, anyway?

Roger Sorting through our files. I've made an appointment with the solicitor.

Joanna Good grief. What now?

Roger Just to draw up our wills.

Joanna That'll be fun.

Roger Well, we've ignored it, because there's really no one to worry about but us. It should be simple. Just a couple of bank accounts and ISAs. And I've still got some premium bonds. I need to list both our assets, in case you go first.

Joanna I think we've established that I won't.

Roger Well, when it happens to me, I want all our financial affairs to be in order, so you're able to get on with your life, maybe find someone else.

Joanna OK.

Roger Even a brief show of reluctance would have been nice.

Joanna In the words of Ricky Nelson, there'll never be anyone else but you for me.

Roger I'm so glad we stayed married …

Joanna Are you?

Roger Yes. Yes, I am.

Joanna Well, me too.

Roger Because we've got a substantial property we bought all those years ago, while Peter is now having to split the profits on their house with Sally, and Kirsty hasn't got any capital assets at all so he can probably only afford a one-bedroom flat! It pays to stick together.

Joanna No other reason why you're glad we stayed married?

Roger Ermm … It helps that you're ageing quite well. Easy on the eye.

Joanna While you're falling apart like a cheap flat pack.

Silence.

Roger What are you doing?

Joanna Just checking the account balance on my running away fund.

END MUSIC

Never Be Anyone Else But You – Ricky Nelson

Choose from our freshly cooked
menu of delicious dishes

Fresh roast chicken and garden vegetable wrap,
in delicious sauce, with chips

Pan roasted butternut squash with artichokes,
potato gnocchi and sage _It's_
butter or chips _plural, not_
possessive!

Pork katsu curry burger, with onion rings on a
toasted <u>brooch</u> roll and chips
What???!!

Chargrilled minute steak with ~~sorted~~
mushrooms and chips _sautéed_

Beef noodles, with sauce and chips

Let's Spend the Night Together

OPENING MUSIC
Forever Young – Bob Dylan

SCENE 1: *Breakfast time. Joanna is in the kitchen, stacking toast. Roger enters.*

Joanna Do you know what day it is?

Roger Yes. I also know the name of the Prime Minister and the capital of Italy. Do you want me to list animals beginning with F? Or recite the alphabet backwards?

Joanna This is not a memory test … Well, it sort of is …

Roger It's February the fourteenth, OK?

Joanna And that is …?

Roger When the car insurance is due.

Joanna Hilarious.

Roger Look, I know it's Valentine's Day. And, had I forgotten, your heart-shaped toast is a bit of a clue.

Joanna Is it in your inside pocket?

Roger What?

Joanna The card. I don't seem to see one about your person.

Roger Very perceptive. There isn't one.

Joanna Why? I don't ask for much!

Roger Hah! You make more demands than the taxman.

Joanna Can't you be romantic for one day?

Roger I am *incurably* romantic!

Joanna In a zipped-up, stoic, emotionally constipated way?

Roger Just because I don't go on about it.

Joanna That's certainly true.

Roger The strong and silent type, that's me.

Joanna Behind every strong and silent type is an awful lot of quiet.

Roger You want noisy declarations of love?

Joanna Of course I do!

Roger We go through this every year. We're married. We're not illicit lovers, nor are we yearning with unrequited passion.

Joanna Sometimes I am. When you're up all night, watching cricket.

Roger Valentine's Day cards are *anonymous* expressions of desire (and we know each other) to an unattainable love object (which you're not), sent, mostly, by spotty losers (which is definitely not me).

Joanna You forgot to get a card, didn't you?

Roger I don't need my thoughts expressed in a commercialised, saccharine sentiment, created by an algorithm in some factory in Slough. I'm perfectly capable of telling you how I feel without shelling out three-fifty to Hallmark.

Joanna Go on, then.

Roger OK. Whenever I see you, sound fails. My tongue
falters. Thin fire steals through my limbs, an inner
roar. And darkness clouds my ears and eyes.

Joanna Sounds like you're coming down with flu.

Roger I'm poleaxed by passion. It has similar symptoms.

Joanna Is that how you feel about me?

Roger Intermittently.

Joanna Or is it how Catullus feels about Lesbia?

Roger Steal from the best.

Joanna And by golly, you did. This came for you.

She slaps a card on his chest.

Roger Just the one?

Joanna One more than you deserve.

Roger Who can it be from?

Joanna Try and work it out.

Roger Carrie in the greengrocer's winked at me the
other day …

Joanna She has a detached retina.

Roger The handwriting's familiar. Who's the bird on the
front?

Joanna Dorothy Parker, of course.

Roger [*reads*] 'Oh life is a glorious cycle of song. A
medley of extemporanea. And love is a thing that
can never go wrong … [*both together*] And I am
Marie of Romania.'

They laugh.

Roger Very nice. Thank you. Right. That's Valentine's
Day done, then. Coffee?

Joanna Not so fast! Where are my roses?

Roger In the garage.

Joanna Well, go and bring them in.

Roger The garage on the bypass.

MUSIC BREAK

(I Never Promised You a) Rose Garden – Glen Campbell

SCENE 2: *Living room. Next morning. Joanna's on the phone. Roger enters.*

Roger [*calls out*] I'm off!

Joanna [*puts her hand over the phone and mutters to Roger*]
Wait a mo. On the phone. [*back to caller*] Sorry, yes. I
will get the paperwork to you. Promise. I'm just
trying to find all the receipts ... No, I don't want a
penalty! ... Right. Thanks so much. Bye. Love you!

Roger Who was that?

Joanna Tony Watson.

Roger Our new accountant?

Joanna Yes.

Roger Who we've only met once, in his office? Nervous
cough? Bitten fingernails?

Joanna That's him.

Roger And yet you signed off with 'Love you'.

Joanna What?!

Roger To our accountant. You said, 'Bye. Love you.'

Joanna Did not!

Roger Yes. You did!

Joanna I don't even know him.

Roger My point.

Joanna So why would I say that?

Roger Again, my point. But you say it to most people.

Joanna Maybe, people I know and like but not …

Roger 'Fraid so. You've turned a corner. You're now telling complete strangers you love them.

Joanna It's just automatic. I don't really think about it.

Roger Well, you'd better start, because right now, he's staring at the phone wondering if you want him for more than just his spreadsheet.

Phone rings.

Roger Oooh. That'll be him. He's had a think. He's going to try his luck and ask you out to lunch.

Joanna No, it'll be Sally, wanting to come round because it's *The Christening* today. [*answers phone*] Hello? Oh, really? Well, thank you, but … I can't today … because … Must go. I'm just seeing my husband off. Goodbye. And thank you for calling.

Roger laughs.

Roger Told you. Nice try, giving him the brush-off, with the belated formality but it's too late. The flame is lit.

Joanna I thought I was quite firm.

Roger Exactly. That's a come-on. Treat 'em mean, keep 'em keen just makes you more desirable. Look at me. I'm still hanging in there. Determined to win your affection.

Joanna You might have more chance of success if you'd got me a card yesterday.

Roger And you shouldn't have said you were seeing me off. It sounded like you were telling him you'd be alone. He'll be round, with his calculator.

Joanna Oh, stop it! I can't be rude, can I? Because I might lose him.

Roger Hasn't stopped you being rude to me.

Joanna Well, I can always get another husband but a good accountant is hard to find.

Roger And on that bombshell, I'm outta here. See you later.

Joanna OK.

Roger You could plead with me to stay and protect you.

Joanna You're the honorary godfather. You've got to show up at the christening.

Roger Come with me.

Joanna Don't want to.

Roger Are you sure?

Joanna Yes, very sure.

Roger You've known Peter even longer than I have.

Joanna But you shouldn't be going, either.

Roger He's my friend.

Joanna Was. Then he left his wife. Our friend …

Roger You have to move on. He's got a new family now and babies unite people.

Joanna Sally wants to kill him and so do I. She'll be round soon and I'll spend the day listening to the many ways Peter has broken her heart and ruined her life. But you go and have a nice time with the cheating ratbag.

Roger She seems to have moved on, actually.

Joanna	How do you know?
Roger	I was behind her while she was getting petrol yesterday.
Joanna	When you went to get my roses?
Roger	She was in this van from the garden centre, sitting in the passenger seat. The driver got out, leaned in her window and gave her a kiss and then went to the checkout. She saw me in the wing mirror, jumped out, gave me a massive hug and said she was loved up.
Joanna	Crikey! That was quick! She was sobbing on the phone to me on Wednesday, saying her life was over.
Roger	He sent her an invoice inside a Valentine card, apparently. I might try that next year. For services rendered …
Joanna	What's he like?
Roger	Tall, beefy man of the soil. Dungarees, muddy boots, slight stoop. Called Ted. Apparently, he cleaned out her pond and then offered to landscape her borders …
Joanna	Can you ditch the *Carry On* innuendos?
Roger	'Ditch'? I see what you did there.
Joanna	Did you talk to him?
Roger	No, she wouldn't let me. Said it's early days.
Joanna	Why didn't you tell me this when you got home?
Roger	She asked me not to say anything. She thinks you won't approve.
Joanna	But she always tells me everything. Even when I don't want her to.

Roger   She wouldn't have told me if I hadn't seen him
         kiss her.

Joanna   Right. I'm coming with you.

Roger   Where?

Joanna   To the christening.

Roger   Why?!

Joanna   I was boycotting it in solidarity with my jilted
         friend, but she obviously doesn't need me any
         more, now she's got Gabriel Oak.

Roger   Why don't you stay here and have lunch with
         your fawning financial adviser?

Joanna   I'll be five minutes.

Roger   I'm not waiting!

Joanna   Make it fifteen, I've got to shower …

Roger   I'm leaving now!

Joanna   Really? Are you happy with that shirt?

Roger   Deliriously.

Joanna   It's old and tatty.

Roger   It's vintage and well worn, like me.

Joanna   The top button's about to come off.

Roger   I don't need a top button. I'm not wearing a tie.

Joanna   You have to wear a tie in church.

Roger   No you don't. Peter said it's very informal.

Joanna   His whole life's informal. Remember when he
         wore cycling shorts to the opera? Aren't those
         your gardening trousers?

Roger   I occasionally wear them for light weeding duties …

Joanna   Put on something proper!

Roger   These are proper.

Joanna   They're just baggy chinos.

Roger   I want them loose, so I have some air around my sorely knee.

Joanna   Your knee is fixed.

Roger   I still get twinges.

Joanna   Well, it's a long drive. Don't go, then.

Roger   I'm definitely going to this christening.

Joanna   You look as if you're going to a barbecue.

Roger   Maybe I am. There's a 'do' afterwards. Could be in the garden.

Joanna   It's February. Are those trainers?

Roger   You've had plenty of time to verbally abuse my wardrobe. Why are you suddenly having a go just as I'm walking out of the door?

Joanna   Because you'll be with me now and I want you to look as if you've made an effort.

Roger   Oh, trust me, it'll be an effort.

Joanna   Come upstairs with me.

Roger   No time for that!

Joanna   I want you to get my hat box down, after you've changed.

SCENE 3: *Joanna is driving along the motorway. Music is playing on the car radio: Chuck Berry, 'Riding Along in my Automobile'.*

Joanna   Oh, perfect!
She turns up the volume. Roger, who had nodded off, wakes up suddenly, deafened by the volume.
Roger   What?! Where are we?!

Joanna   Sorry, I didn't know you'd nodded off. Great
driving song, eh?

Roger   Can't hear you. I think my eardrums have burst.

Joanna   All right, turn it down, then. I don't mind. Much.

Roger   How're you doing?

Joanna   Bored. Motorways are so dull. It's not proper
driving, is it? It's like being on a conveyor belt,
where you hurtle along and then get spat out at
intervals. Same gear, same view of the backside of
a Hyundai. I need a travel sweet.

Roger   Righto.

He gets the tin out of the glove box.

Joanna   No yellow or orange ones!

Roger   Keep your eye on the road.

Joanna   I am. And the view hasn't changed for … 44.8
miles.

Roger   Here you go.

Joanna   Can you put it in my mouth? No, don't! It's
green!

Roger   You didn't say 'no green ones'.

Joanna   Aren't there any red ones left?

Roger   You ate them all when we went to Wales.

Joanna   It is your job to replace the sugar-free gum and
the travel sweets.

Roger   The travel sweets aren't empty.

Joanna   They are if there are no red ones!

Roger   Do you want this green one or not?

Joanna   You have it.

Roger   Don't want it.

Joanna Well, put it back in the tin, then.

Roger You licked it!

Joanna Doesn't matter. It's only us that eats them.

Roger I'll get some more when we get off the motorway.

Joanna Only get the tin with all red ones. I think they're called Forest Fruits. There's an empty tin down there somewhere, you can check …

Roger Watch out! Everything's slowing down.

Joanna All right! I can see!

Roger It must be a breakdown or something. But at least it's moving.

Joanna No, it's not. All the brake lights are coming on. We're now in a car park. If only you'd let me make some sandwiches!

Roger That would have taken another half-hour. It's your fault we're stuck. If we'd left when I wanted to, we wouldn't have hit this traffic.

Joanna You don't know that.

Roger I do. I can see a breakdown truck ahead, up the hill.

Joanna That dog's staring at me.

Roger He heard the word 'sandwiches'. [*pause*] What does the satnav say about this traffic?

Joanna Congestion ahead. Leave at next exit.

Roger And that, ladies and gentleman, is the winner of this week's award for stating the bleedin' obvious.

Joanna Next exit is 3.6 miles!

Roger That should only take us …

Joanna About an hour! Maybe more! Because nothing's damn well moving!!

Roger Told you not to come.

Joanna Unless you can find any red sweets, don't speak to me. I'm upset.

Roger You hide it so well. Shall we try a bit of soothing Radio 3?

Joanna No thanks.

She turns car radio music up: 'Highway to Hell', AC/DC.

SCENE 4: *An hour later. They are sitting at a café table in a service station.*

Joanna It's a nice touch, that they have pens and drawing paper for the children.

Roger Not just the children.

Joanna What are you doing?

Roger Making a few corrections to the menu.

Joanna Oh, here come the Apostrophe Police.

Roger It's not just the apostrophes, it's more lies and damned lies. It says here – and we believed them – 'Fresh roast chicken and garden vegetable wrap, in delicious sauce.' But in fact … it's …

Joanna Let me see what you've written. 'Polyfilla, wrapped in wallpaper'?

She laughs.

Roger Wait! I've been too kind. Give me the other menu.

Joanna Someone will see you defacing café property.

Roger Doubt that. Took them fifteen minutes to notice we were here.

Joanna Show me. 'Puke in Amazon packaging.' Mmmm, sounds yummy.

Roger An accurate description of what I just sent back, to what's laughingly called the kitchen – three microwaves and a stack of frozen boxes.

Joanna He looked surprised you hadn't finished it.

Roger And very nervous, when he stuttered 'Everything all right for you guys?' and then shot through the door before I could tell him it perishing well wasn't!

Joanna I'm sure part of their training is 'Don't wait for an answer'.

Roger You think they're *trained*?

Joanna I'm glad I just had the cheese sandwich. They can't really mess that up.

Roger But somehow they managed it. Didn't you find a thumbprint on the cheddar?

Joanna Must be the chef's signature dish.

She laughs.

Roger No wonder they make you pay when ordering.

Joanna Cripes! Look at the time! We really shouldn't have stopped.

Roger I had to get you off the road. You turn into Dick Dastardly when you're hungry.

Joanna Thank you, Muttley. Let's go.

They get up, push the chairs back and walk out through the service station.

Joanna Oh, shouldn't we get a christening present?

Roger Here?! The choice is a three-foot meerkat or a neon paddling pool.

Joanna   Isn't there a proper jeweller's?

Roger   Oddly, Cartier's research showed there wasn't a huge demand for a branch at Clacket Lane services.

Joanna   We should take something.

Roger   It's OK. I've opened a savings account for him.

Joanna   You didn't tell me.

Roger   You aren't remotely interested in anything to do with this baby.

Ping of text received.

Roger   Ah. Peter's sent me a picture of Hermes.

Joanna   We'll get the giggles when they say that in church.

Roger   He's captioned it. 'Waiting for my Godfather'. He's smiling. Look.

Joanna says nothing.

Roger   What?

She is becoming tearful.

Roger   What's the matter?

Joanna   You would have made a wonderful dad. I'm so sorry it didn't happen …

Small silence.

Roger   Give me the keys.

Joanna   Are you feeling all right?

Roger   I should be asking you that.

Joanna   I meant are you OK –

Roger   Well, I think I've got food poisoning but …

Joanna   – to drive? Is your knee holding up?

Roger   Soon find out … Oh, there's the gents'. I'll just nip in.

Joanna   Again?

Roger In case we hit more traffic.

Joanna I'll see you back at the car. Bye.

She starts to walk away.

Roger Bye! Love you!

She calls back.

Joanna What?

Roger You heard.

MUSIC BREAK

I Think I'm Going Back – Dusty Springfield

SCENE 5: *Half an hour later, driving along Surrey lanes. Roger is at the wheel.*

Roger [*sighs*] Oh, what NOW!

Joanna There's a tractor up ahead. And a caravan behind it. Just seen them going round the bend.

Roger Maybe our Mensa satnav can suggest a quicker route?

Joanna Says 'You are on the fastest route', and arrival two forty-five.

Roger That's too late. It'll be over.

Joanna We'd better phone Peter.

Roger No point. He'll be at the church already, sorting things out.

Joanna I can't believe there's so much traffic on these little roads.

Roger Probably tourists. It's an Area of Outstanding Natural Beauty.

Joanna   How do you know?

Roger   Just passed a sign. The Surrey Hills.

Joanna   Oh, my gosh!

Roger   What's the matter?

Joanna   I thought it seemed familiar. We've been here
         before, haven't we?

Roger   Yes but not since—

Joanna   [*cuts in*] Not since we came back from India ...
         forty years ago?

Roger   And the rest! Nearer fifty.

Joanna   That was such a special time, wasn't it?

Roger   I'm surprised you can remember any of it.

Joanna   [*excited*] Leith Hill! See that sign? We walked up
         to the top and there's a kind of castle there and
         it was so cool up there, after India ... So fresh ...
         Abinger Hammer! Look! Somewhere here is the
         Silent Pool. You took me to that. It wasn't silent
         while we were there!

Roger   You stripped off and swam in it, you complete
         hippy!

Joanna   England smelled so different from India. So subtle
         compared to the heady perfume from all those
         flowers round the Maharishi's platform.

Roger   I don't think that was the smell of flowers.

Joanna   Everyone was so ...

Roger   Out of it?

Joanna   Happy. So happy. Especially the Maharishi.

Roger   Not surprised, with all those superstars booking in
         for B&B.

Joanna	Don't you love talking about those days?
Roger	We have. Many times.
Joanna	Think back and back and back. To that night …
Roger	Not again!
Joanna	Come on, it's lovely, remembering. Better than playing I Spy … I was sitting on the veranda.
Roger	You were lying down, with that moody Welsh poet …
Joanna	He was quite … Celtic, wasn't he?
Roger	Declaiming all over the place …
Joanna	He was very influenced by Dylan Thomas.
Roger	He looked more like Terry-Thomas, after he fell over the incense burner and knocked his teeth out.
Joanna	And you suddenly walked out of the darkness, towards me. I thought I was hallucinating.
Roger	Which was a definite possibility.
Joanna	I had been doing a lot of heavy meditating, and strangely I was thinking about you, so I wondered if my mind was playing tricks and you were a mirage …
Roger	Like Omar Sharif in *Lawrence of Arabia*.
Joanna	But you were attached to a flame-haired, Pre-Raphaelite Geordie, who said she was your girlfriend …
Roger	She wasn't. We were just on the same flight.
Joanna	She was hanging on your arm, very possessively.
Roger	Too vain to wear her glasses, I was her guide dog.
Joanna	We hadn't seen, or spoken, for two long years …

Roger   No mobiles or social media in them days, lass.

Joanna   It seemed like for ever.

Roger   Your fault. After five days together, you upped and
said you were going to San Francisco, which I
didn't take personally at all.

Joanna   Everyone went to San Francisco that year.

Roger   No, everyone didn't. Just hippies with trust funds
and no work ethic, who could swan about in
cheesecloth and bangles while the rest of us had
to earn a living.

Joanna   You could have come with me.

Roger   I'd just got a job, on the paper.

Joanna   It would have been a good story.

Roger   I was a sports reporter. Anyway, you didn't ask me
to come with you.

Joanna   You know why. I was much too young to make a
commitment.

Roger   Yes, I got that, thank you very much. But you
might have told me, instead of leaving a note
saying 'It's been groovy'. Please!

Joanna   If I'd said I thought I loved you, that would
have been a commitment – especially, if you'd
said you felt the same, wouldn't it? We were
teenagers. Don't think either of us wanted that,
at the time.

Roger laughs.

Roger   We usually have this dangling conversation after
two bottles of wine.

Joanna   And we never remember it the next day. Much

nicer to say things when you're side by side in the car.

Roger   What *things* did you want to …? Take your hand off my knee, madam!

Joanna   Did you? Feel the same? From the beginning?

Roger   You know I did. I was sorry you left, certainly. Very sorry. And I had a feeling of complete joy when I saw you at Rishikesh.

Joanna   You didn't look joyful. You looked slightly cheesed off and you just said …

Roger   'Of all the gin joints …'

Joanna   No, you said, 'Have I missed the Beatles?'

Roger   And you said, 'I think John's meditating somewhere. And half the Beach Boys and Mia Farrow are still here.' Quite briskly, like an information desk, but slightly muffled as you were still underneath the Welshman.

Joanna   I couldn't tell if you were pleased to see me.

Roger   I wasn't sure I was.

Joanna   That was true karma, meeting again. It would have been a complete tragedy if we'd never got back together.

Roger   On the plus side, I might have spent my life happily shoving Bags for Life in the drawer without being told to fold them nicely.

Joanna laughs.

Joanna   Gosh, that was a long week, wasn't it? We hardly spoke.

Roger   Wasn't much to say, was there? You spent most

of your days curled up at the raggedy-toed,
rope-sandalled, prehensile feet of Tom Jones, or
whatever his name was.

Joanna Hywel.

Roger Oh, yes. And he did. At the moon, mostly. In Welsh.

Joanna You were making a lot of noise with that girl.

Roger Just trying to make you jealous.

Joanna Were you?

Roger We were releasing our chakras. It took a while, in
that heat.

Joanna Remember that couple who wanted to take the
Maharishi back to Weybridge?

Roger I think that might have been George Harrison
and Pattie Boyd.

Joanna No, he was captain of a golf club and wanted
the Yogi to hand out the cups at the Annual
Prizegiving.

Roger Yes, I know. I mentioned that in my copy.

Joanna You didn't write about me, in your dispatches
from the ashram.

Roger I did. 'There was this gorgeous bird, who I
dreamed of, even when I was awake, but who
ignored me and made me cry in my sleep.'

Joanna I didn't see that.

Roger Because I didn't file it.

Joanna I wanted to stay on but I had to get back for my
mum and dad's silver wedding anniversary.

Roger So you said. To Hywel. In a very loud voice, so I'd
overhear.

Joanna It worked. You suddenly had to go back, too.

Roger I'd only had a week to get the story …

Joanna Had you *really*, or did you just say that so we could fly back together?

Roger Why would I do that, when you'd barely looked at me?

Joanna I hated that red-haired hippy but I wanted to be her, because you always had your arms round her.

Roger I was trying to hold her up when she was stoned.

Joanna Celeste.

Roger What?

Joanna Celeste Astra. That was her name, wasn't it?

Roger No, it was Janice. She got very confessional, after a smoke. Janice Gamage.

Joanna I wonder what happened to her?

Roger I don't.

Joanna Were you sad they didn't seat us next to each other, on the plane?

Roger I told them not to. I said we weren't together. Didn't want to sit next to you for nine hours.

Joanna Why not?

Roger Because I would have found it impossible to resist the urge to drop back the seat, drag you on to my lap and ravish you until the bloke behind complained that he wanted to put up his tray table.

Joanna laughs.

Joanna Why didn't you say that, at the time?

Roger How would that have helped get us through the flight?

Joanna   I thought I'd lost you at Heathrow but you were waiting for me …

Roger   I was waiting for my baggage.

Joanna   I was so excited when you asked if I wanted a lift to town …

Roger   Actually, *you* said, 'I've got no money. I don't know how I'm going to get back.'

Joanna   You had that kinky Morgan car.

Roger   Beautiful ash frame.

Joanna   A hysterectomy over every bump. But you didn't head for London …

Roger   No sense of direction.

Joanna   We went down the A30 and we started winding around those country roads, through beautiful villages … Going nowhere, for hours.

Roger   You didn't object.

Joanna   I was very, very happy.

Roger   Every time I looked at you, you were smiling, your hair blowing all over the place, like a golden storm. That was when I realised … Because you didn't ask for the hood up, or rummage around for a scarf, like most girls.

Joanna   Believe me, I wanted to, but I was channelling Françoise Hardy.

Roger   That explains the Gauloises.

Joanna   And you had that Zippo lighter and whizzed it down your jeans till it struck. So sexy. Achingly cool.

Roger   I just can't help myself.

Joanna I wanted to stay in that car with you for ever but the sun was setting and we drove down this spooky road, with the tree roots spilling out and the branches arching overhead, like Treebeard and we … [*she suddenly shouts with excitement*] Stop!

Roger I can't stop, there's a car behind me.

Joanna Well, pull into this lay-by, because … this is it!

Roger This is what?

Joanna This is where we were. Friday Street. Go back! Go down that road!

Roger I think I'll wait a bit. Not the easiest place to do a U-turn in this traffic.

He switches off the engine.

Joanna Oh, my gosh! I can see the scary trees. It's all still here.

Roger And so, remarkably, are we.

Joanna It's extraordinary, how we just happened upon it …

Silence.

Joanna *Did* we? Just happen upon it …? Or did you arrange to bring me here? As a wonderful surprise?

Roger I think you might be confusing me with a romantic event planner.

Joanna You did, didn't you?

Roger Well, it was Valentine's Day … recently.

Joanna Did you ever intend to go to the christening?

Roger Yes, I did! Until you decided to come. I knew that was not a good idea.

Joanna   I wouldn't have caused a scene.

Roger   You might. When I showed you the baby picture, you
          were very upset. Couldn't risk it. So I called Peter.

Joanna   When?

Roger   When I went to the loo, at Clacket Services. I said
          the traffic was appalling and I wouldn't make it.

Joanna   You're right. That photo ... Started me thinking
          about what might have been, if I hadn't run away,
          to San Francisco.

Roger   You left so fast, there were scorch marks on the
          carpet.

Joanna   I told you, I'd arranged to meet everyone there. I
          couldn't let them down.

Roger   You'd just let me down.

Joanna   I was very confused. My head was all over the
          place.

Roger   The mantra of the serial bolter.

Joanna   I was hoping that I could forget you.

Roger   By bonking someone else?

Joanna   I didn't bonk someone else. Well, not for nearly a
          year. Because ... I realised I was pregnant. Seven
          weeks after I left you.

A long silence.

Roger   You were pregnant with my baby, is that what
          you're saying?

Joanna   Yes.

Roger   And what happened to it? Did you get rid of it?

Joanna   No. I had a horrible miscarriage. You know about
          that.

Roger I know you had a miscarriage but I thought that was … much, much later. A year, maybe. Some random lover …

Joanna I blurred the timelines.

Roger You could have told me, when we met in India.

Joanna Oh, really? It's hardly a chat-up line, is it? 'Oh, hi, I was pregnant with your baby but I miscarried. Nice to see you.'

Roger is silent.

Joanna I'm so sorry, darling.

She starts to cry.

Joanna Look, when I was told … we were both told … that the complications of the miscarriage meant I could never have children, I couldn't tell you then, because … it was years later and I was afraid you would hate me.

Roger I don't hate you. I'm just desperately sad you carried this with you all this time. We could have grieved together.

Joanna But I was a long way from you, from home. And I felt so guilty, because it was my fault. I left you when I wanted to stay with you and I partied like crazy, in California. I didn't look after myself, or the baby. Not like Kirsty did.

Roger Kirsty?

Joanna Yes, you told me how careful she was with her diet and not drinking and she had a beautiful, healthy baby and I didn't … She did all the things I should have done.

Roger   But you didn't know you were pregnant.

Joanna   No excuse. Our baby died because I was a reckless, stupid teenager.

Roger   If you'd known you were pregnant, with my baby, would you have wanted to keep it?

Small silence.

Joanna   Honestly? Possibly not. Because I thought I had years and years to have babies, when I was older. But when I lost it, everything shut down. For months, I could hardly speak. I did a terrible thing. You wouldn't ever be a father if you stayed with me.

Roger   So Kirsty's baby made you want to tell me?

Joanna   Yes … Because it feels like … we're going back, somehow, to where we were. And you have a right to know, which is more important than me being scared of telling you.

Roger   Oddly, I think I did know – or at least suspected – but I didn't think it would help to question you about it and I was so … dazzled by you –

Joanna   We were dazzled with each other.

Roger   – nothing else mattered. Not even kids. All I wanted was you. I should have begged you not to leave, which is what I wanted to do. It's my fault as well.

Joanna   None of it's your fault. I ruined your life.

Roger   Oh, don't be ridiculous. Of course you didn't. Hold tight. Gap in traffic. I'm turning round.

Roger starts the engine and swings the car round, turning into

Friday Street.

Joanna   If I could time travel back, I would have stayed with you.

Roger   You have stayed with me and having no children means we give all our love to each other. Although I think, percentage-wise, I've always been the major donor, while you ... Not so much. Nothing but take, take, take ...

Joanna sniffles.

Joanna   I'm so lucky to have you.

Roger   Yes, you bloody are.

Joanna   Do you want to go home now?

Roger   Certainly not. Now, blow your nose. Recognise this pub?

Joanna   Oh, of course! This is our place. Where we really began. That was our room, over the porch ...

Joanna's phone rings.

Roger   Is that the amorous auditor?

Joanna   Yup.

Roger   He thinks you're home alone.

Joanna   Hey, why don't I accept the call and let him hear us snogging?

Roger   In a pub car park? No thanks. Put me down, woman!

Joanna rejects the call. Ringing stops.

Joanna   Spoilsport. Do you want to go in, for a drink?

Roger   Got a better idea.

Joanna   Oh?

Roger   Let's spend the night together.

Joanna That's exactly what you said to me in nineteen
sixty-eight.

Roger I know. Fancy a spot of déjà vu?

END MUSIC

Dance Me to the End of Love — Leonard Cohen

Good session yesterday. Loved the shark story. Who knew you could scare them by clapping? I'm almost done with the South China Sea. Just tidying up the storm sequence. Need more info. Were you hunkered down below decks? (As if!) Or did you strip off and lash yourself to the mast? I think the readers would like to visualise it. Or maybe it's just me! Night, darling!

Rix! I need you to get back to me! You haven't gone wreck diving again, have you? Looking forward to hearing you speak at the Royal Geographical Society next week. What's the dress code for an explorer's 'plus one'? Should I wear leather shorts and a bush hat – or channel my inner Raquel Welch and rock up in a fur bikini? xxx

Sorry. Missed your call. Was in the shower. Will you ring me when you get back from Madrid, so we can have a proper talk about the Tenere desert chapter? I should warn you I'm looking for a little more emotional input. You need to be honest about your feelings. Explain later. Xx

Working My Way Back to You

OPENING MUSIC
The Things We Do for Love – 10cc

SCENE 1: *In the kitchen. Elevenses time. Roger has just taken a phone message and Joanna has come in from the garden.*

Roger How's it going out there?

Joanna I hate ground elder! It's strangling the rhubarb.
And the borage is going berserk.

Roger Dig a hole –

Joanna I have!

Roger – stick in an arrow and point it towards Andy and
Sarah's garden.

Joanna Don't think I haven't thought of that. I'm being
targeted by malevolent foliage.

Roger On the plus side, we haven't got Japanese
knotweed.

Joanna Yet! But the bamboo's sneaking through, from
Mandy's. I think we need to put in a root barrier
by the fence.

Roger Good idea. I'll sort it.

Joanna No, you can't do it, with your knee!

127

Roger My knee's been replaced.

Joanna But you still mustn't dig.

Roger You can't do all the gardening.

Joanna I think we have to face the fact that this garden is a bit too much for us. We need to get it landscaped. Make it easier to manage. We should get Sally's new bloke to do it. He's a gardener.

Roger Landscaping costs a fortune. Even mates' rates. Coffee?

Joanna Yup. Thanks. In a big mug, please. I'm parched.

Roger Oh. Esther just phoned.

Joanna Who?

Roger Your ex-editor.

Joanna Cripes! Rolling back the years. But … I've got my mobile here. She didn't ring me.

Roger She phoned the landline.

Joanna Why? Nobody phones the landline. [*realises*] Oh, she thought you might pick up – and you did.

Roger She asked how you were and wondered if you'd like a job.

Joanna What did you tell her?

Roger I said, 'No woman of mine goes out to work. I keep her barefoot in the bedroom to service my insatiable desires …'

Joanna laughs.

Joanna What did Esther say to that?

Roger There was a huge pause and then, in a voice about two octaves lower she said, 'Lucky her.'

Joanna She's had a crush on you ever since that book

launch at Kensington Roof Gardens, when we had a power cut and you thought she was me.

Roger   How was I to know you'd sprinted towards the bar as soon as the lights went out? Not a word of farewell!

Joanna   No time to waste. They were limiting the drinks but I thought they wouldn't be able to see me properly in the dark.

Roger   Devious doesn't begin to cover it.

Joanna   I think devious applies more to you than me. I only left you for five minutes …

Roger   I didn't think you *had* left me, that was the point. I reached out for you, in the dark. It was quite a turn-on.

Joanna   Those were early days for us.

Roger   We snogged almost constantly.

Joanna   Not always each other, as it turned out.

Roger   Easy mistake to make.

Joanna   Really? I'm surprised you didn't notice the difference immediately.

Roger   What difference?

Joanna   Esther's got rather thin lips. Severe. Not like mine. Must have been like kissing a clothes line.

Roger   I don't remember finding it unpleasant. If her lips were slightly unyielding, I probably put it down to the fact that I must have done something to upset you and you were clenched.

Joanna   They weren't *my* lips! Remember? Also, she's only five foot two. You must have stooped.

Roger   As I recall, she pulled my face down, towards her.
          I did think that was rather unlike you. But we
          were constantly trying new things …

Joanna   When the lights came back on—

Roger   [*cuts in*] I saw you, suddenly floodlit, approaching
          at speed, armed with martinis.

Joanna   You looked terrified, shoved Esther away and said,
          'Jeez!'

Roger   I regret that. It was rather unkind.

Joanna   I was going to throw the drinks at you but then I
          thought …

Roger   What a waste?

Joanna   Yes, I did think that but … It had all been quite
          fun up till then – you and me – and suddenly I
          thought, 'He's mine! Get off!' I was so angry!

Roger   You looked pretty scary. Hair flying. Medusa of
          the Martinis.

Joanna   Then you said to Esther, 'I'm so sorry, I thought
          you were someone else.'

Roger   Again. Rather cruel. Not proud of that.

Joanna   Well, it made me laugh. And almost cry at the
          same time.

Roger   Poor Esther.

Joanna   Did she mention it? Just now on the phone?

Roger   Oh, yes. We reminisced about our intimate
          moment of instant passion. She said her lips were
          still burning at the memory.

Joanna   Hilarious.

Roger   Of course she didn't mention it! After nearly fifty years, I think we've both got over it.

Joanna She hasn't. She's always carried a torch for you.

Roger Pity she wasn't carrying one that night, it would have saved a lot of embarrassment. Still, could have been worse …

Joanna How?

Roger After three martinis, I could easily have turned to my left and snogged Keith Waterhouse.

They laugh.

Roger I do remember the walk back to yours being rather … interrupted.

Joanna We took a short cut, through those dark, narrow mews. Old-fashioned lamp-posts … soft lights …

Roger Where you took advantage of me. More than once.

Joanna I couldn't let you go …

Roger Because you were holding me up.

Joanna Well, yes, but I realised just how awful it was, seeing you with someone else – even if it might have been a mistake.

Roger It was definitely a mistake!

Joanna Still, I rather enjoyed your continuous efforts to reassure me!

Roger I went through most of the Grovelling Apology/ Making Amends tips in my How To Keep Her Happy manual. It was exhausting. At one point, I think I had to sit down.

Joanna You fell down.

Roger I remember the smell of camomile …

Joanna   You landed in someone's flower trough. They knocked on the window.

Roger   And we ran away like schoolkids.

Joanna   Stumbling on the cobbles.

They giggle like schoolkids.

Roger   I guess we have poor Esther to thank, for that *very* hot night.

Joanna   She may not be thrilled to hear that.

Roger hands Joanna a piece of paper.

Roger   Oh, here's her office number.

Joanna   I thought she'd retired.

Roger   Got headhunted. She's working for a small publishing house. An offer she couldn't refuse. She'll fill you in. I said you'd ring her back.

Joanna   OK. I'll call her later.

Roger   Do it now! I want to know what she wants.

Joanna   Tough. I've got to have a bath first. I'm covered in mud.

Roger   Do you want me to come up and scrub your back?

Joanna   It's not my back that's dirty.

Roger   What's that got to do with anything? Oh, don't forget your coffee.

Joanna   Why don't you bring it up?

MUSIC BREAK

Give a Little Bit – Supertramp

SCENE 2: *The living room, an hour later. Joanna enters. Roger is dozing on the sofa.*

Joanna Well, this is really interesting. After all these years, she ... [*she pauses*] Are you asleep?

Roger [*yawns*] What? No! Just resting my eyes.

Joanna So what have I just said?

Roger You started to tell me ... [*he pauses, feeling his way carefully*] about your phone call with Esther?

Joanna Lucky guess!

Roger Simple deduction. You said you were going to call her.

Joanna I hate it when you're right.

Roger I aim to irritate. So ...?

Joanna She sends her love, of course.

Roger I don't want it.

Joanna I know but she suggested we all meet up for dinner in town one night.

Roger What did you say?

Joanna I was non-committal.

Roger Good. I can only handle one love-struck, besotted babe at a time.

Joanna Who's the other one? [*she laughs*] She's quite determined to get together. With you. I might have to say you've got acid reflux. Or cataracts.

Roger Why?

Joanna It makes you sound less attractive.

Roger You'll have to try harder than that! So what about this job?

Joanna Esther's running the autobiography division.

Roger And she wants you to write mine?

Joanna I think *she'd* want to do that. No, she thought I might like to edit one.

Roger Which one?

Joanna Rix Roden's.

Roger Who's he?

Joanna You know! He's always on TV, living with ancient tribes, swimming in the Arctic, running across the desert. He climbed K2. He's very well known.

Roger He's a celebrity. You said the reason you gave up editing was because the publishing world was no longer interested in proper authors …

Joanna That was true.

Roger And you were fed up with being asked to rake together the ungrammatical ramblings of vacuous celebrity airheads. Four fifths of One Direction being the last straw, you said.

Joanna And I meant it. But Rix has achieved things.

Roger Rix. What kind of stupid name is that?

Joanna I can tell you what it's short for.

Roger Hatrix? Baldricks? Scalextrics?

Joanna Asterix.

Roger Ha! So he's named after a short, fat comic-book character?

Joanna His father knew the writer.

Roger Even so, that's a very cruel thing to do to a child.

Joanna And it's not even his first name.

Roger Which is …?

Joanna	Homer. But that was way before *The Simpsons.*
Roger	Homer Asterix. I actually feel sorry for him.
Joanna	He's also an environmentalist. Knows David Attenborough.
Roger	Doesn't everybody?
Joanna	Grew up in Cairo, father an archaeologist, he's got interesting stories and he's articulate, so Esther says.
Roger	Why can't he write it himself, then?
Joanna	He has. But every writer needs an editor, as you know.
Roger	So Esther's talked you into it, has she?
Joanna	She just said he's quite high profile and he needs a … mature editor.
Roger	Brave of her to use the 'M' word.
Joanna	I think in this case, it means intelligent, not old. She said my name came up and she thought I'd be perfect and it was worth giving me a call to see if she could persuade me.
Roger	And has she?
Joanna	I said I'd go and meet him.
Roger	Where? In the sand dunes of Namibia?
Joanna	At his home. It's an eco house, top of a Cumbrian mountain. He's very self-sufficient.
Roger	Of course he is.
Joanna	So I'm going there on Thursday. Bit of a schlepp. He has got a London base but I thought it would be more interesting to see this place first.
Roger	You'll probably find him out in the fields, scything

barley in a torn shirt.

Joanna You're being a bit churlish. I thought you'd be pleased for me.

Roger I am. You're a fantastic editor and you should do it.

Joanna Let's just find out if I like him first!

MUSIC BREAK
Tired of Waiting – The Kinks

SCENE 3: *Three days later, early evening. Roger is cooking in the kitchen. Joanna crashes in.*

Joanna I need a large drink!

Roger Green tea? Cranberry juice?

Joanna What?! No! Wine, of course!

Roger But it's one of our non-drinking days.

Joanna [*through gritted teeth*] I don't care.

Roger So, if we have a drink tonight, shall we move our non-drinking day till next Monday? Only tomorrow is Friday and we're going to Di and Al's, so we can't not drink there, can we?

Joanna Shut up! Just give me some wine.

Roger OK. But three dry days a week was your idea, so let's just put it on record that you were the one who cracked, not me.

Joanna Stupid, fatuous, egocentric idiot!

Roger That's a bit harsh! I'm just looking after your health.

Joanna I'm talking about Rix Roden.

Roger So you didn't hit it off, then?

Joanna Understatement.

Roger I wondered why you were back so early. Why didn't you ring?

Joanna No signal on the train.

Roger Well, I'm just making a lonely omelette. Want me to double it?

Joanna S'OK. I'm not hungry.

Roger All right. Go on, then. Tell me …

Joanna Wine first, please!

Roger [*pouring*] Say when.

Silence. He keeps pouring.

Roger I said say—

Joanna [*cuts in*] I heard you.

He hands her the wine.

Roger Just the half pint, then.

Joanna Leave the bottle.

Roger What happened, for goodness' sake?

Joanna Well, I finally trekked up the damn mountain. More of a small hill, as it turned out. Bragging from the start, I should have heard warning bells.

Roger I thought he was picking you up from the station?

Joanna So did I. But no sign. So I got a lift from a builder's van.

Roger Was he out when you got there?

Joanna I thought so. Rang the bell. No answer. Rang it again. Finally, this tall, tousled figure opened the door. Six foot two-ish. Green eyes, black hair.

	Wearing nothing but running shorts. Navy silk, with a white trim –
Roger	You hardly noticed.
Joanna	– and a sleeveless, black, crew-neck Calvin Klein vest, which was very, very damp …
Roger	Nice attention to detail.
Joanna	He was sweating and I thought he must have been working out but he said, 'Yes? What do you want?', as if I was collecting for something. And I told him I was his editor and he said, 'You're a day early. It's tomorrow. I know it's tomorrow. I'm calling Esther!' and shot off. And then, in wandered this woman in a satin slip and I told her who I was and she said it was her fault he'd forgotten about me. Turned out she was Saskia, his fourth ex-wife, and she'd just come round to discuss access rights for the children and that was two days ago and this was the first time they'd got out of bed.
Roger	Well, it all sounds good copy for the autobiography so far …
Joanna	He came back in and said, 'This is actually bloody inconvenient,' and I said, 'It's bloody inconvenient for me, too! And if this is how you greeted your previous editors I'm not surprised you're running out of options.' And I stomped out.
Roger	But you were up a mountain?
Joanna	Yup. I didn't really think it through, cos I also needed a pee but I could hardly go back in and ask to use the loo …

Roger   He didn't follow you and offer you a lift?

Joanna   No, he didn't, but fortunately there was a bus at the bottom of the hill, going to the station.

Roger   Still, it's good to know that they've revived their relationship, don't you think? For the sake of the children, if nothing else. It'll make a heart-warming chapter in the book.

Joanna   I don't care about the bloody book and I don't care about him! Wasted journey. And these shoes are ruined.

He gives her a hug.

Roger   I'm sorry, darling. Why don't you go and have a bath? The omelette's ready, so if you don't mind, I'll just …

Joanna takes the plate from a surprised Roger.

Joanna   Oh, thanks!

Roger   Hey, I thought you weren't hungry.

Joanna   I am now.

Roger   OK. Fine. I'll make myself another one.

Joanna   I don't know what he thought he was trying to prove.

Roger   That he had a terrible memory for dates?

Joanna   No. He knew I was coming. He just wanted to shock me, or disconcert me. I don't know what he wanted to do but …

Roger   But he succeeded.

Joanna   No, he didn't! I walked out.

Roger   Well, good for you. I'm sorry you had to go through that.

Joanna He's just another spoiled superstar.

Roger Do you want me to have a word with him?

Joanna About what?

Roger Upsetting my woman.

Joanna He's a karate grandmaster.

Roger I've done a bit of tai chi.

Joanna It's not the same.

Roger I'm not scared. I'll challenge him to a duel.

Joanna laughs.

Roger What's funny?

Joanna Well, you talk big but you're wearing a pink pinny and whisking eggs.

Roger One twirl and I become a superhero!

Joanna Omelette Man?

Roger *Il tuo dolore è il mio dolore.*

Joanna And that means ...?

Roger Your pain is my pain. It's from *The Godfather.*

Joanna Is it?

Roger Not sure. But it sounds good, doesn't it?

Joanna Yes. It does. Thank you for offering to bash Rix Roden but it won't be necessary because I won't be seeing him again.

Roger Are you sure?

Joanna Why would I want to work with him? He's behaving just like any other jumped-up celebrity. He's the reason why I left publishing. I'll go and call Esther. Tell her it was a complete disaster and I'm not doing it.

Roger Aren't you going to finish this omelette first?

Joanna No, it's OK. I'm not hungry. You have it.
Roger Oh. Thank you so much.

MUSIC BREAK
Days Like This – Van Morrison

Phone Shane
RE windows
- inside and
out!!

SCENE 4: *Later that evening. In the bedroom. Joanna enters.*
Roger is in bed, reading.

Joanna There you are! I didn't realise you'd gone to bed.
Roger Why wouldn't I? It's nearly midnight. Have you
been on the phone to Esther all this time?
Joanna Pretty much.
Roger How long does it take to say 'No'?
Joanna Well, we talked about a lot of things …
Roger You told her what happened?
Joanna Yes, I did. And she said Rix had phoned her up,
with profuse apologies, wanting my address to
send flowers …
Roger And you told her to tell him where to stuff them?
Joanna [*guiltily*] Sort of.

Roger [*dawning comprehension*] You didn't say no, did you?

Joanna I did, at first. But then Esther told me that he'd been assigned three other editors before me and he couldn't work with any of them and she got a bit tearful. She said he's a very big name and she didn't want to lose him and he told her he thought he could really work with me …

Roger How does he know? He only saw you for about two minutes?

Joanna That's what I said. But she said he's a very good judge of people. And he felt we had a connection …

Roger Like the one he has with his ex-wife?

Joanna Apparently, he just liked me. Is that so hard to believe?

Roger Of course not!

Joanna He seemed sincere.

Roger How do you know how he seems? You're only getting this through Esther.

Joanna Well, we had a quick Zoom.

Roger What?!

Joanna Esther set up a video conference call and it was really good to hear his thoughts and talk about what he was hoping to achieve.

Roger And what was he wearing?

Joanna A rather dramatic cashmere bathrobe that had been woven by Tibetan monks. Why?

Roger laughs.

Roger I know you so well.

Joanna Oh, stop it! You seriously think I'd be tempted by a hunky, mountaineering ex-soldier and former rodeo rider, who has wrestled bears, lived with headhunter tribes in New Guinea and skied across the Himalayas?

Roger When you put it like that, I realise my fears are ridiculously unfounded.

Joanna And he can dance a mean salsa.

Roger He can salsa?!

Joanna He was on *Strictly* last year. Remember?

Roger Remarkably, no, I don't.

Joanna He had a fling with his dancing partner. They were spotted kissing in a back passage in Soho. That's what ended his fourth marriage.

Roger You'd better watch yourself, then. He sounds as if he puts it about a bit.

Joanna If I'd been so easily swayed by every attractive man I've ever worked with, obviously I'd have left you years ago.

Roger That's comforting.

Joanna But to quote Olivia Newton-John, 'You're the one that I want.'

Roger Say that again in a black leather jumpsuit and I'll believe you.

Joanna Look, this is just work.

Roger So it *is* going to be work. You didn't say no, you said yes!

Joanna Not immediately! But Esther offered me considerably more money …

Roger Money isn't everything.

Joanna No, but it's useful if we want to landscape the garden.

Roger Right. So if you're earning the big bucks now, does that make me a kept man?

Joanna Do you want to be?

Roger What are the perks?

Joanna Shift up and I'll show you.

Roger Oof!

MUSIC BREAK
Don't Get Me Wrong – The Pretenders

Take lasagne out of freezer.
DO NOT
FORGET!

SCENE 5: *In the garden, a week later. Mid afternoon. Joanna breezes in. Roger is sitting in a chair with one leg up.*

Joanna Hi, sorry I'm a bit late.

Roger A bit?!

Joanna I would have left earlier but Rix wanted to show me his mountaineering equipment.

Roger Doesn't he have any etchings?

Joanna Funny. We got quite a lot of work done.

Roger Oh, good. And how is Indiana Jones?

Joanna I'm having to be quite strict with him.

Roger Oh. So he has tried it on?

Joanna In the edit. He has a tendency to waffle and he's obsessed with facts. For instance, we don't need to know exactly how many strokes he did each day when he rowed across the Atlantic, do we?

Roger I certainly don't.

Joanna Just an average – ten thousand – will do, I told him. But he says he needs readers to know how tough it was.

Roger How tough he is, you mean.

Joanna He's certainly Action Man. He was in the forest when I arrived.

Roger Karate chopping down trees?

Joanna Quite the opposite. He'd just planted two hundred and fifty oak saplings.

Roger And what's he doing this afternoon?

Joanna Don't be tetchy. I've said I'm sorry I'm late. Hey! Why've you got your leg up?

Roger Just resting it.

Joanna Did you have a fall?

Roger Ah! I often wondered when 'Did you fall over?' becomes 'Did you have a fall?' Now I know.

Joanna What have you done?

Roger I just … dug that root barrier in. That's all.

Joanna What?!

Roger And I might have tweaked my knee.

Joanna   That's crazy! I thought you were going to ring Ted?

Roger   I left messages, but I think they've gone away and it's not a big job.

Joanna   But you're not supposed to put pressure on your knee. Digging is the worst thing. Especially as you haven't had it checked out properly since the op. You could have done serious damage!

Roger   Bamboo roots are very shallow, so I didn't dig deep. And I did it in stages.

Joanna   You shouldn't have done it at all.

Roger   Why not? I'm not an invalid.

Joanna   Well, you are at the moment.

Roger   It's just a twinge.

Joanna   I could have done it!

Roger   I don't want you to do it. OK? I wanted to do it. Myself. And I did. So. Where's the paracetamol?

MUSIC BREAK
Mercy, Mercy Me – Robert Palmer

Milk and Bananas
- not over-ripe
like last time

SCENE 6: *In the kitchen, four days later. 10 p.m. Joanna is on the phone.*

Joanna   Here's my point: you've sketched over the women in your life a bit. You have to be more open about your feelings, not just what you've done ... [*she laughs*] Do I? Who? Oh, really? Well, thank you. One other thing I'm concerned about is making readers feel they're there, with you. When you describe these expeditions, these challenges, your writing tends to be a bit matter of fact. I think we need to talk about how it affects you. Do you ever cry? Doubt yourself? [*beat*] No? Thought not. [*she laughs*] Oh, well. Worth a try. We'll discuss it all tomorrow. You too, sweetheart. Sleep tight. Bye ...

She hangs up the phone, sees Roger.

Joanna   Oh! Cripes! You made me jump! What are you doing, lurking?

Roger   I'm not lurking. I am standing in my own home, wondering if we could finish dinner at last.

Joanna   Sorry. You know what authors are like.

Roger   No. I only know about musicians. And even the demands of the Rolling Stones seem quite reasonable compared to him.

Joanna   Oh, he's all right, really.

Roger   All right? You just called him sweetheart. And he was a stupid, fatuous egotist a couple of weeks ago.

Joanna   He paid me a lovely compliment. He said I

147

reminded him of the most important woman in
his life.

Roger His mother?

Joanna No! His first wife. She was killed in a car crash in
Greece. She was pregnant, although they didn't
know it. I don't think he's ever got over her,
which is why he keeps getting married, trying to
find her again.

Roger Fascinating. More goulash?

Joanna No thanks. I'd better go and make some notes on
what we've talked about.

Roger I didn't think we talked about anything much,
these days.

Joanna I don't mean us. I mean Rix and me.

Roger Oh, I know what you mean.

Joanna Look, I'm sorry if I'm a bit preoccupied but this is
my first editorial job in a while and I want to do
it properly.

Roger Fair enough. But surely he knows about the nine
o'clock rule.

Joanna The one you made up?

Roger I didn't make it up. It's a truth, universally
acknowledged, that you don't phone anyone after
nine o'clock unless it's an emergency; and you
certainly don't talk till ten – ten fifteen, in fact!
Doesn't he have anyone at home who's as cheesed
off as I am?

Joanna He's between wives at the moment. Although
Saskia seems to be hanging around.

Roger   Probably waiting for him to stop talking to you.
Saskia and I are both at a loose end. Maybe I
should call her and take her out to dinner?

Joanna   Yes. Why don't you?

Roger   You really wouldn't mind?

Joanna   Why should I?

Roger   You wouldn't be a tiny bit jealous?

Joanna   Jealous?

Roger   Yes. Remember we were talking about how angry
and possessive you felt when I accidentally kissed
Esther?

Joanna   That was in nineteen seventy-one.

Roger   So you cared in nineteen seventy-one but you
don't care now?

Joanna   You're not going to kiss Saskia, are you?

Roger   Who knows where the evening may lead.

Joanna   This is daft talk. She doesn't even know you exist.

Roger   At the moment, I'm not sure you do, either.

MUSIC BREAK
Roxanne – The Police

Please remember
to pick up my red
dress from the
cleaners this time!
Here's the ticket

SCENE 7: *The living room, an hour later. 'Roxanne' is playing and Roger is having a drink. Joanna enters.*

Joanna I've finished the notes. But you didn't have to wait up.

Roger I wasn't. Just having a quiet drink. On my own. As usual.

Joanna Why are you playing that?

Roger What?

Joanna That song.

Roger What song?

Joanna 'Roxanne'.

Roger Oh, that. It's a good song.

Joanna A song about a marriage in trouble.

Roger Is it?

Joanna You know it is.

Roger If you say so. I just asked Alexa to play some seventies hits – and this is one of the tracks that came up.

Joanna Are you sure?

Roger Am I sure about what?

Joanna That's what you did? Asked Alexa?

Roger Positive.

Joanna It's a miracle.

Roger I'm quite good at technology.

Joanna Are you?

Roger You know I am. I can re-boot the router, replace the ink in the printer …

Joanna And yet you didn't notice we haven't got Alexa any more?

Roger   Hilarious.

Joanna   I'm serious. We haven't got Alexa. We got fed up with her spying on us and gave her to your goddaughter. Remember?

Roger   Ermm … I could have sworn …

Joanna   Busted, mister!

Roger   OK. Fair cop.

Joanna   So why are you playing 'Roxanne'?

Roger   You're lucky I'm not playing 'Ruby, Don't Take Your Love to Town' …

Joanna   I told you, it's just work. I'm fed up with this. I'm going to bed.

Roger   Fine. See you in the morning. Oh, wait, I probably won't. You'll be off at sparrow's fart to meet Brix, or whatever his name is.

Joanna   I do have to leave early. Oh, don't forget to take the lasagne out of the freezer for tomorrow night.

Roger   Single portion?

Joanna   I'll be home for supper. Could you call Shane and ask him to come and clean the windows?

Roger   Already have.

Joanna   Oh, good. And will you rinse out the recycling bin? It's pretty manky.

Roger   Rinse out the bin? That's way below my pay grade.

Joanna   Well, I think that's just about it.

Roger   [*quietly angry*] I think that's just about it, too.

MUSIC BREAK
Go Your Own Way – Fleetwood Mac

I'll be late
tonight.
Don't wait up

SCENE 8: *The bedroom, thirty hours later, 8 a.m. Roger comes in with a cup of tea.*

Roger   Cup of tea. Don't knock it over.

Joanna yawns.

Joanna   Oh, thank you. That was a lovely idea last night, supper in bed.

Roger   Best lasagne ever.

They laugh.

Roger   Although pavlova for afters was less of a success.

Joanna   I know. The meringue pinged everywhere. Still got some in my hair.

Roger   Very crunchy. It was like sleeping on the beach.

Joanna   Just like the old days.

Roger   When we were at home together every evening ...

Joanna   Oh, don't spoil it!

Roger   Sorry. [*he climbs back into bed*] Yes, it was wonderful. Waking up together, as well, instead of hearing the door slam as you shoot off to meet Iron Man.

Joanna So make the most of me while I'm here.

Roger Again?!

Joanna We won't be disturbed. Rix is on his way to Scotland.

Roger Is he running there?

Joanna laughs.

Roger So, what time shall we set off?

Joanna Are you giving me a lift to the station?

Roger What do you mean?

Joanna Ermmm … You first. What did *you* mean when you said, 'What time shall we set off?'

Roger We're meeting Marion and John at the Leaping Hare for dinner tonight, remember?

Joanna No, I don't remember.

Roger Their fortieth wedding anniversary. Dinner with friends who were there on the day. Like us.

Joanna She didn't call me.

Roger No, because John's made it a surprise for her. He called me. I told you. You said 'yes'.

Joanna But that was before …

Roger Before Indiana Jones swung into your life?

Joanna Yes, it was before that and I'm on a deadline for this edit. As you know.

Roger You still have to eat. Surely you can manage an evening with some of our oldest friends?

Joanna Not this evening. I'll call them later and explain … Marion works. They'll understand.

Roger   They might. I won't.

Joanna   It doesn't stop you going tonight. I just … can't.

Roger   Why?

Joanna   Because … [*deep breath*] I'm going to meet Rix in Inverness. [*she hurries on*] I told you …

Roger   You did not!

Joanna   I was just about to. Waiting for the right moment.

Roger   That was never gonna come. Are you heading on up to Gretna to get married? He seems to do that quite often. Although I don't remember us getting divorced.

Joanna   Look, he knows I'm a swimmer and he's swum across the Hellespont and in the Arctic. He wants me to go and swim in Loch Ness with him to get … the feel of things.

Roger   And exactly what 'things' does he want you to get the feel of?

Joanna   Oh, stop it! It's a great opportunity. And it will be useful for the book.

Roger   Is that all it is?

Joanna   Well, it's exciting. It's an adventure!

Roger   It's inconvenient.

Joanna   I'm sorry. It has to be now, because next week he starts training for the Marathon des Sables, which is this huge run across the Sahara—

Roger   [*cuts in*] I know what it is. Doesn't he ever spend the day with his feet up, bingeing on Netflix?

Joanna   Rix says we should all break down seemingly impossible barriers. Push ourselves to the limit.

Roger   Well, he's certainly pushing me to the limit.

Joanna   I'm sorry to hear that.

Roger   Swimming in a loch? It's bloody dangerous!

Joanna   I've done lots of open water swimming ...

Roger   At this time of year?

Joanna   I'll be with someone who knows what he's doing.

Roger   Oh, I'm sure of that.

Joanna   He'll look after me.

Roger   I think that's my job.

Joanna   OK. You can come. You don't have to swim. Stay in a hotel.

Roger   And where will you be? In a tent, with Crocodile Dundee?

Joanna   I'll have my own tent.

Roger   You seriously expect me to think this is just to help with the writing of the book?

Joanna   Yes. It's relevant to understanding him, his motivation.

Roger   Oh, I understand him – and his motivation.

Joanna   You think he's lured me up there? That I'm ... what? Having an affair with him? Or going to?

Roger   Are you?

Joanna   It's flattering but he's young enough to be my ... cousin. He can choose any woman he wants, why would he choose me?

Roger   I chose you. So I completely understand why anyone else would.

Joanna   Thank you. And I chose you. Remember? And this is just ...

Roger   Just work. Yeah, so you keep saying.

Joanna It is! He's doing a challenge. He wants to swim the length of each Scottish loch …

Roger I don't care what he wants. He's not doing it with you.

Joanna But …!

Roger No buts. Last night was the only evening we've been together for a fortnight. Is that why you came home and were so nice? To soften me up for today's blow?

Joanna That's horrible! I'm not a calculating bitch!

Roger Surely you can see how it looks. You only come home to change your clothes – to go back out and meet him.

Joanna It's just …!

Roger Work? They don't look like work clothes.

Joanna If you're talking about Thursday …

Roger I'm talking about most days.

Joanna He was doing a talk at the Royal Geographical Society and he invited me. It was formal.

Roger So that would last till, what? Eight thirty?

Joanna And there was a small reception afterwards.

Roger Nine? Nine thirty?

Joanna And we were hungry, so we popped into the Savoy Grill …

Roger Ten thirty? Eleven, max?

Joanna And some people joined us …

Roger And kept you talking till two a.m.?

Joanna They had some very interesting stories. About him. It's important that I was there.

Roger   Your friends – people you love, who love you –
are more important than a celebrity narcissist and
his sycophants! Tonight, you're coming out with
me.

Joanna   That's a bit James Bond.

Roger   That's what you want, isn't it?

Joanna   As long as it's the Sean Connery Bond, obviously.

She laughs. Roger stays stony.

Joanna   I was being funny.

Roger   I don't think it's funny. Admit it. You want
someone who can sweep you off your feet
without putting his knee out. Don't you?

Joanna   Maybe I do.

MUSIC BREAK

Best of Both Worlds – Scott Walker

SCENE 9: *The kitchen, two hours later. The phone rings. Roger
answers.*

Roger   Hello?

Joanna   It's me.

Silence.

Joanna   Say something.

Roger   You first.

Joanna   OK. I'm really, really sorry.

Roger   How's the monster? And I'm not talking about
Nessie.

Joanna   I didn't go to Scotland. Rix has done his back in.

157

Roger   Say that again?

Joanna   He's hurt his back. Can't move. In a lot of pain.

Roger laughs long and hard.

Joanna   That's not very nice.

Roger   Oh, it is. Very nice indeed. Was he sobbing when he phoned you? I do hope so.

Joanna   He didn't phone me. I phoned him to tell him I was *not* going to Scotland. I want you to know that.

Roger   Honestly? He didn't phone you first?

Joanna   Yes. Honestly. I got on the train, but on the way to town I realised that I should put Marion and John first. So I rang him and he said he was about to call and tell me what had happened but he had to wait for the excruciating pain to subside. He could hardly speak.

Roger   He doesn't know what pain is till he's had a knee replacement.

Joanna   That's what I told him. I said you were really brave and stoic.

Roger   Did you?

Joanna   No. But I thought it. When I heard him whimpering.

Roger   What a jessie!

Joanna laughs.

Joanna   So I can make it to the dinner tonight.

Roger   Sadly, dinner's off. John's got a dodgy stomach, so they've switched it to next week.

Joanna   Oh, poor John.

Roger   So, I'll see you shortly? Great.

Joanna   Well, look … erm … I'm pretty sure I can tie
up this edit and do the rest by email, so as I'm in
London anyway I might as well go and see Rix,
check a few things and then come home.

Roger   I thought he was a gibbering, incoherent wreck?

Joanna   He is at the moment and he needs time for the
painkillers to kick in, so I'll have lunch with
Crazy Liz and then spend a couple of hours with
him. Maybe you can rustle up something lovely
for supper?

Roger   Again? I'm getting tired of being a kept man.

Joanna   No, you're not. See you later. Love you!

Silence.

Joanna   Say something.

Roger   Don't be late.

MUSIC BREAK

Is She Really Going Out with Him? – Joe Jackson

SCENE 10: *The kitchen, much later that evening. Joanna enters.*

Joanna   Hi, so, *so* sorry I'm late …

Roger   [*brightly*] No worries!

Joanna   I couldn't get away.

Roger   Never mind.

Joanna   And I had to switch the phone off …

Roger   Obviously. That's fine! I understand.

Joanna   So I guess supper's ruined …?

Roger No, it was delicious. Fish pie. Your favourite.

Joanna Any left?

Roger 'Fraid not. I had a call from Esther.

Joanna Esther? Why?

Roger She couldn't get hold of you, so she phoned me and said Rix told her that you'd pretty much finished the edit so she'd like to drop off a very good bottle of champagne for you, as a surprise.

Joanna Oh, that was nice …

Roger I said you'd be home shortly, so why didn't she join us for supper?

Joanna You didn't send me a message to tell me?

Roger There's a clue in the word 'surprise'.

Joanna Cripes! You haven't seen her for years, have you?! Don't you think she's looking a bit … [*whispers*] elderly?

Roger She looked pretty good to me. Hasn't changed much at all. Her hair's still blonde.

Joanna You are so naïve. Did you manage to get rid of her?

Roger No. We had a bottle of rioja and chatted. Time passed – very pleasantly – but you still hadn't shown, so I decided we needed to eat. I opened a nicely chilled sauvignon blanc with the fish and after that … ermm … Oh, yes, we had a massive snog and then I put her in an Uber and she went home. [*silence*] So, how was your evening?

END MUSIC

I'm Not in Love – *10cc*

160

Kirsty's mother's just called looking for you. Are you still at the marquee? Apparently the roses in the floral arch are the wrong kind of pink! I was seriously tempted to tell her to 'get a life' but I said 'I don't think flower arranging is part of the Best Man's duties. Call the florist.' She said 'You're one of Peter's friends, aren't you? You all seem very assertive!'

I totally agree with her! Especially when you're wearing your dominatrix spike heels

Which I am ... Wanna come upstairs and check them out? Xx

Slight hitch. Kirsty's stupid brother has locked himself in. Broken his keycard in half. Tempted to think he'll be no great loss but I'm with the locksmith at the moment. Chairs in marquee still damp after rain last night. Could you go and check they've wiped them down?

Not in these heels!

I can't do everything! It's ten minutes to kick-off

I am a guest. In a peach silk dress. I am not going to flick round a duster!

Thanks for nothing!

Heartbreak Hotel

OPENING MUSIC
The Things We Do for Love – 10cc

SCENE I: *Day 1, early afternoon. Roger and Joanna are driving up the driveway of a very smart country hotel.*

Joanna   This is rather lovely. It looks a bit *Alice in Wonderland*, don't you think? Or that painting *The Badminton Game*, with all those giant trees … Wow! There's a wisteria that's nicely tamed.

Roger   What does that mean?

Joanna   Nothing. I just know you're always wrestling with ours. Maybe we should have a word with their gardener?

Roger   I can control my own wisteria, thank you very much.

Joanna   Honey-coloured stone. Very warm and welcoming. We can park over there, can't we?

Roger   Yup. It says 'residents' and that's us.

Joanna   The forecast is good for tomorrow. No rain. Very little wind.

Roger   Well, that's handy, as we're eating in a tent.

Car stops and engine off. Roger groans, stretches.

Roger   Aarrgghhh … My body's seized up.

Joanna   Long drive. But there's a pool here. We can have a swim.

Roger   What a shame, I didn't pack my trunks.

Joanna   [*swiftly*] I packed your trunks.

Roger   [*resigned*] Oh, goody.

They open the car doors and get out.

Joanna   There's the marquee! Do you see? By the trees.

Roger   You can hardly miss it.

Joanna   It's rather beautiful. What would you call that colour?

Roger   Mud?

Joanna   No, it's more … terracotta. And lovely blue banners. Hey! What does it remind you of?

Roger   A very posh version of the tent Sally and Peter got married in in Nepal, in nineteen eighty-two.

Joanna   Exactly. That's a bit weird, don't you think? That they chose that?

Roger   Kirsty's parents organised the wedding, not Peter. And Kirsty wasn't born when Peter married Sally, so she's not going to know the tent's the same colour, is she?

Joanna   It's not a good omen.

Roger   Thank you, Mystic Meg, but I don't see a problem. Peter and Kirsty have got a baby together now …

Joanna   Baby? He's nearly three!

Roger   Never!

Joanna You should know. You're Hermes' honorary godfather.

Roger He's not called that any more. Peter said he couldn't pronounce his own name –

Joanna laughs.

Joanna Or didn't want to.

Roger – so he calls himself Joe.

Joanna Smart kid. Shades of Zowie Bowie.

Roger opens the car boot.

Roger Blimey! Three cases?

Joanna That's not a case, it's my hatbox. I'll leave it in the car for the moment.

Roger OK. You take the small bag. Otherwise known as 'mine'.

Crunching on gravel as they take stuff out of the car.

Roger And I'll take this ... crikey! What's in here?

Joanna Just my wedding outfit.

Roger Is it chain mail?

Joanna You guessed. I was hoping to upstage the bride.

She laughs.

Roger And why hasn't this case got wheels?

Joanna They went wonky. Look, I can take the big case, if it's too much for you ...

Roger OK. You're super fit. I get it. Just allow me to do blokes' things, now and then – even if it puts me flat on my back for a month.

Joanna Fine. Carry it yourself.

Car doors slammed. Locked. Crunching as they walk towards the hotel entrance.

Joanna   Peter wouldn't have wanted all this fuss, would he?

Roger   He's doing it for her, that's fine. She's not some tired old divorcee.

Joanna   You mean she's not someone his age?

Roger   I do, yes. She's a young woman and she wants to be a bride in a big frock.

Joanna   Stop being so nice and understanding!

Roger   Look, Sally's happy with Ted. And if Sally's not bothered about Peter getting married again, nor should you be.

Joanna   I'm not, really. It's just … Let's face it, we're only here cos you're best man. Godfather, best man … Hasn't he got any other friends?

Roger   Not many, after he split with Sally. I wanted to do it – although I'm a bit out of practice.

Joanna   Probably the last time you were best man was Peter's first wedding. Remember we spent their wedding night with them, in that filthy bus in Kathmandu?

Roger   Kirsty and Peter's wedding night will be a bit more upmarket, in the bridal suite here.

Joanna   It's practical. After a long day, you don't want to travel.

Roger   You sound like your mother.

Joanna   You were quite firm with her, when she tried to persuade us to get married in a place like this.

Roger   I just said I didn't fancy sharing my wedding night with family and friends.

Joanna	She was quite cross. She liked getting her own way.
Roger	I'm saying nothing.
Joanna	She looked so glum in the wedding photos.
Roger	She told me she thought Chelsea Register Office was very downmarket.
Joanna	She thought you were quite downmarket as well. Long hair. Smelly Afghan sheepskin coat …
Roger	But for the wedding I got a tailor-made, rather sharp Lord John suit.
Joanna	Pretty cool.
Roger	Even so, your father glared at me as if I was abducting you.
Joanna	We couldn't get away fast enough, could we? Whizzing off in your crazy car …
Roger	My beautiful Morgan. Nought to sixty in 4.5 seconds …
Joanna	We almost upended your sister, jumping in front of us trying to catch my bouquet.
Roger	Chased down the Kings Road by a police car. Couldn't catch us.
Joanna	But you stopped, anyway – and we didn't get done for speeding.
Roger	Thanks to you. Not even those heartless rozzers could bring themselves to hand a ticket to a sobbing bride. Who're you waving at?
Joanna	No idea. But they're waving at us. Might be Kirsty's brother.

Roger stops.

Roger   I might have to put the case down for a minute.

Joanna   It's just up here.

Roger   Oh, no! Steps!

Joanna   There's a ramp.

Roger   Doesn't make it any easier, cos there are no wheels.

Joanna   Look, there's a nice man with a luggage trolley coming towards us.

Roger   I'll sit on it and you can carry the case in.

Joanna   Sadly, I think you mean it.

They continue, through swing doors into the hotel foyer.

Joanna   Gosh. This is very *Country Life*.

Roger   All in the best possible taste, as your mother would say.

Joanna   Kirsty's mum and dad have made sure of that, even though they had to cut the guest list down.

Roger   Few arguments there, Peter said. Lairy Uncle Jerry didn't make the cut.

Joanna   Peter really likes him but he tap dances on tables at family dos, apparently.

Roger   Sounds like our kind of guy.

Joanna   I know, but her parents are much more sensible than we are. Even though they're younger than Peter.

Roger   And us.

Joanna   I'd love to know what they really think about their only daughter marrying a Senior Railcard holder.

Roger   I'm sure they're just pleased she's marrying someone she loves.

Joanna   Do you think they'll be as happy as we are?

Roger   Oh, we're happy today, are we?

Joanna   What do you mean?

Roger   Well, yesterday we were definitely not happy. At least, you weren't. I got the silent treatment all day for not noticing your new hair colour.

Joanna   That's just marital badinage.

Roger   Is that what it is?

Joanna   Yeah. Doesn't mean, deep down, I'm unhappy with you …

Roger   Phew!

Joanna   At least, not all the time.

Roger groans. Joanna laughs.

MUSIC BREAK

*I Knew the Bride (When She Used to Rock and Roll) –
Dave Edmunds*

SCENE 2: *Their hotel room, an hour later. They are putting the key in the door.*

Roger   This better be worth all the hanging about.

Joanna   Stop moaning. This is one of only two superior deluxe suites and they gave us tea and cake while they got the room prepared for us.

Roger   What does that mean?

Joanna   We'll see, shall we?

Hotel-room door opens. They enter.

Joanna   Now that's a huge improvement!

Roger   [*puzzled*] Is it? Tell me why.

Joanna   The bed's in a nicer position …

Roger   Than what?

Joanna   Space either side. And the wardrobe's got sliding doors. And look! We've got a lovely view of the parterre gardens.

Roger   So, can I put the bags down?

Joanna   Let me just check the en suite …

Roger   I'd better get a big tip for this.

Joanna   It's lucky we came the day before the wedding, so we had a choice of rooms.

Roger   And we've been in every one of them!

Joanna   I don't know why you're so grumpy.

Roger   It's not easy to keep a smiley face when I have walked at least three miles down these endless corridors, weighed down by twenty kilos of wheel-less Samsonite!

Joanna   You didn't have to carry it!

Roger   It seemed wise to keep the case with us when I had no idea what room we'd end up in. Still don't.

Joanna   We've certainly been upgraded. The shower is much better placed and the mirror is well lit …

Roger   So we're staying?

Joanna   I *think* so …

Roger   Not good enough. I need your final answer. Is this the room – which looks exactly like all the others – where I am, at last, going to put down our bags?

Joanna   Hmmmm … I'll just try the bed …

Roger   No, you won't! Step away! The beds are all the

same. Look at me! I'm letting go. The bags are
released. They're on the floor! Touchdown!

Roger puts the bags down and then notices the bed.

Roger For crying out …! What is that?

Joanna Where?

Roger On the bed!

Joanna Oh, rose buds.

Roger Why?!

Joanna They make people happy.

Roger Tearing the heads off roses and flinging them on a
duvet makes people happy? What kind of people? It's
floral genocide! I'm tempted to call the R.H.S. …
Flaming Nora!

Joanna What now?

Roger Have you seen this?

Joanna They're guest towels.

Roger How can you tell?

Joanna It's obvious.

Roger Even when they have mangled them into …
mating squirrels?

Joanna They're swans. Entwined. Obviously. There's the
beaks. It's quite clever, don't you think?

Roger No. It's a criminal waste of human resources.
And … good grief! Here's a cliché. Heart-shaped
chocolates on the pillow!

Joanna Bedtime treat.

Roger I don't want food on my pillow. You fall asleep on
those and wake up thinking you've grown a giant
mole overnight.

Joanna Look, they've left us a bottle of bubbly.

Roger It's pink!

Joanna I don't care what colour it is. Pop it open.

Roger There's a card with it.

Joanna Let me see.

Roger Don't snatch! I can read! It says, 'Congratulations! Wishing you a wonderful … celebration!'

Joanna That's … kind.

Roger Stone the crows! You know what's happened?

Joanna Could you stop spitting feathers and pour the drinks?

Roger This is the bridal suite! Explains all the dead roses, chocolates and pink stuff. This will be Kirsty and Peter's room tomorrow night! We'll have to move out. They must have got confused. I'll phone reception.

Joanna Just open the bottle …

Roger We can't stay here!

Joanna Yes we can.

Roger But we're not the bride and groom.

Joanna But it is our wedding anniversary.

Silence.

Joanna OK?

Roger Even I know our anniversary was three months ago.

Joanna You know that – but they don't.

Roger They?

Joanna I got so fed up with the rooms they were showing us that I told them it was our wedding anniversary.

Roger   When?

Joanna   When you went to the loo. I said you'd be very
disappointed, because you'd so wanted this to be
a lovely, romantic weekend in a beautiful hotel, as
you'd recently recovered from some … health issues.

Roger   What health issues?

Joanna   Your knee.

Roger   A knee replacement is hardly life-threatening. And
it was eighteen months ago.

Joanna   OK, I laid it on a bit thick but … Hey presto! It
worked. You always get better treatment if it's a
special occasion.

Roger   But it isn't.

Joanna   We'll make it special, as always.

Roger   Just when I think I know what you're capable of …

Joanna   I pull one out the bag!

Roger pops the cork and pours the drinks.

Roger   They could find out you're lying.

Joanna   I don't think they ask for your marriage certificate
any more. Which is a pity. Because there's always
that frisson of the illicit about a hotel room, isn't
there?

Roger   That's because most people come to hotels for
sex, occasionally with the wife.

Joanna   Or someone else's. You should have signed in as
Benjamin Braddock, like you used to. Then they'd
think we were having an affair.

Roger   Only if they'd seen *The Graduate.*

Joanna   The first film we saw together.

They clink glasses.

Roger Here's to you, Mrs Robinson.

Joanna So, here we are, Benjamin.

Roger Yes, here we are, Mrs Robinson.

Joanna Benjamin, would you unzip me, please?

Roger Are you trying to seduce me, Mrs Robinson?

Joanna Would you like me to?

Roger Oh, yes. sure. Thank you. Very much.

Joanna Will you bring me a hanger?

Roger A hanger? Oh – yes. Wood?

Joanna What?

Roger Wood or wire? They have both, Mrs Robinson.

Joanna Either will be fine.

Roger It's a little-known fact that Anne Bancroft was only five years older than Dustin Hoffman when she played Mrs Robinson.

Joanna It's actually quite a well-known fact. Now stop talking and get on the bed.

Roger How long have you suffered from this crippling shyness, Mrs Robinson?

They both laugh but then Roger yelps.

Roger Argh! Bloody roses! Why didn't they choose a thornless variety?

MUSIC BREAK
Floating Away (in a Bath Tub) – Toploader

SCENE 3: *An hour later. Roger and Joanna are in the bath together. Door is open.*

Joanna Do you think we've overdone the bubbles?

Roger Who said that? Is there somebody else in this bath?!

Joanna We should get a big bath like this at home.

Roger Somebody still has to have the tap end.

Joanna No, they don't. You see the taps are in the middle
here. They've thought of everything.

Roger My fingers are getting crinkly.

Joanna Stop fidgeting.

Roger Are you going to get out so I can wash my hair?

Joanna What? No! We're having a nice relaxing wallow.
Together. Sit still.

Roger Trying to but you keep wriggling about.

Joanna Water is a very sensuous element. Charles
Sprawson called it 'the black masseur'.

Roger He was describing doing the front crawl in a
fathomless, blue-black ocean, not sitting in a hotel
bubble bath.

Joanna It slides over you, silky, caressing—

Roger [cuts in] Oi! Watch where you put your feet!

Joanna I'd love a foot massage.

Roger I'm sure you can get one, at the spa.

Joanna I want you to do it.

Roger What?! You said we were having a relaxing wallow.
Now you're giving me a job!

He gingerly takes her heel.

Joanna Cup my heel in your hand. And stop looking like
a Clarks shoe fitter who's just spotted a verruca.

Roger You know I've never been keen on handling feet.
Even when they're as lovely as yours.

175

A sharp knock on the door.

Joanna That'll be room service.

Roger What?!

Joanna I ordered more champagne.

Roger You called room service – and then ran a bath?

Joanna Of course. They usually take ages but they seem to be quite quick here.

Roger But we're in the bath! I'll shout out. Tell them to go away …

Joanna Don't! They'll leave it on the table. They're very discreet.

Roger But the bathroom door's wide open.

Joanna OK. But we're covered in bubbles, so they're not going to see anything.

Roger This is ridiculous!

Joanna Don't get up!

Roger I am going to shut the door, or …

Joanna Or what?

Roger Or it'll be all over the servants' quarters!

Joanna This is not *Downton Abbey*. They've seen it all before … Sit down!

Roger No, I'm getting out … Don't try and stop … God! They need handles on this …

Joanna Put one leg over first.

Roger Argh … cramp!

Room door swings open. Waiter brings in bottle of champagne.

Roger Oh, good evening. Could you put it down right over there, please?

Joanna Thank you sooo much!

Roger   No! No need! Leave it! Sorry, I mean … We'll open it ourselves. When we're ready. So you can just go. *Now*.

Joanna   Thank you *hugely* again. Bye!

Roger   Bye. Lovely sunset!

Waiter exits. Door shuts. Joanna bursts out laughing.

Joanna   You've got your hands crossed over your boy's bits.

Roger   Do you blame me?

Joanna   You realise you said, 'lovely sunset', when you had your bottom turned towards him?

Roger   There are limited conversational options when straddling the bath rim, naked …

Joanna laughs again.

Roger   It's not that funny and I've still got cramp. I can't move.

Joanna   OK. Hang on. Let me climb over you and I'll get out and pull you forward. Put your arms round my neck.

Joanna tries to pull him.

Joanna   Jeeps! You're so slippery! Your top half's already out, can you do a forward roll on the bathmat?

Another brisk knock on the door.

Roger   Don't be ridiculous! Oh, God, what now? Kick the door shut, quick. Don't let go of me!

Joanna   If I don't let go, I can't kick the door shut, can I? I'm just going to grab this from under you …

Roger   Don't take the towel! I need it.

Joanna   I need it more. Bit skimpy but got no choice.

She wraps the towel around herself. The door swings open and the waiter enters with an ice bucket.

Joanna   Hello! Nice to see you again so soon.

Roger   Ahh ... the ice bucket, of course.

Joanna   Essential.

Waiter clears throat.

Roger   My wife will sign for this as she's slightly more ... upright.

Joanna   There you go. Sorry it's a bit damp. Thank you so much ... Neville? Is it? Just looking at your lapel badge.

Roger   I haven't got any small change about my ... person. Sorry!

Neville makes what sounds like a suppressed laugh that turns into a cough, then exits and shuts the door.

Roger   He was stifling a smirk. He couldn't leave fast enough.

Joanna   I'm surprised he didn't offer to resuscitate you, as you're hanging over the bath like a dead pheasant ...

She laughs.

Roger   He probably thought we were trying a challenging new sexual position.

Joanna   Little did he know we did that earlier ... Come on, up you get.

Joanna gets him upright.

Roger   He could be back in a minute. With nibbles.

Joanna   Ooh, hope so. I've worked up a bit of an appetite.

Roger   I bet he'll be on duty tonight in the dining room, giving me a knowing wink.

Joanna   We're not going to the dining room.

Roger   Oh? Found a local restaurant?

Joanna   No, I've ordered room service. We can eat in bed.

Roger   We might make the sheets dirty.

Joanna   I don't care. I'm not washing them.

Roger   And he'll bring it, won't he? Silently sniggering.

Joanna   Possibly, although I'm sure they do shifts …

Roger   I'll be rigid with tension all evening, waiting for the knock.

Joanna   Let's give him something to really talk about. I've got that chain-link belt with me. I can tie you to the bedpost before I let him in.

Roger   Next time, I'm marrying a normal woman.

MUSIC BREAK

Help Me (She's Out of Her Mind) – Stereophonics

SCENE 4: *Late evening. Joanna is in bed, having finished supper. Roger is just coming back to bed after putting the supper trays outside. The door shuts.*

Joanna sighs happily.

Joanna   Mmm … I must have fallen asleep.

Roger   Yes, you did. No fun at all.

Joanna   Where've you been?

Roger   I've just put the food trays outside the door.

Joanna   Oh, good idea.

Roger   Matey was hovering in the corridor with his trolley.

Joanna	He's called Neville.
Roger	No, he's called patronising twerp.
Joanna	I expect he was hoping you'd do something stupid again.
Roger	He smirked, 'I'll take that, shall I, sir?', as if I couldn't put a tray on a trolley.
Joanna	He's only doing his job. [*beat*] Have you got a headache?
Roger	No.
Joanna	Why are you rubbing your head?
Roger	It's nothing. He made me so cross.
Joanna	By offering to help you?
Roger	By being as smarmy as an oil slick. I swung round – quite vigorously – to come back in the room but I didn't realise the door had automatically shut and I banged my head on it. Quite hard. He caught me when I fell backwards and then he used his pass key to let me back in. He held the door open and said, 'We don't want any more accidents, do we, sir?' I could hear him laughing when the door shut.

Joanna starts laughing.

Roger	Don't you start!
Joanna	You're providing so much entertainment, he won't ever want you to check out.
Roger	I'm thinking of making a complaint about his attitude.
Joanna	I don't think helping you up is considered a sackable offence.

Roger   I don't want to talk about it! Lights out?

Joanna   Yes, OK … Sweet dreams!

Roger   Where's the switch?

Joanna   What for?

Roger   The light switch.

Joanna   There isn't one.

She hands him the tablet control for the whole room.

Joanna   Everything's on this tablet. I told you. It controls the lighting, heating, TV, curtains …

Roger   So how do you know which one is lights?

Joanna   There are symbols. For different lights in the room. See?

Roger   No. I'll have to get my glasses …

Joanna   I've shown you all this. Press that one.

The song 'Some Enchanted Evening' starts playing.

Joanna   Not that one! That's the music channel.

Roger   This one …?

An announcer says, 'Hamilton Academicals: three, Heart of Midlothian: nil.'

Joanna   You've switched the TV on! Sports News.

Roger   Well, I wouldn't mind hearing the results …

Joanna   We're going to sleep! Give me the tablet!

Roger   With pleasure. What is the point of making something perfectly simple ridiculously complicated?

Joanna   It's not complicated.

Roger   It's a lot more complicated than a switch. Everybody knows how to use a switch …

Joanna turns off the lights.

Joanna Done it. Goodnight!

Roger Hang on! I'm not properly in bed. I can't see!

Joanna Tough.

A moment's scuffle.

Joanna Stop flinging things around!

Roger Too many pillows!

A clatter as Roger's pillow knocks the phone off the hook.

Joanna What now?!

Roger It's OK. Just knocked the phone. I've put it back. Panic over.

The phone rings.

Roger What's that?

Joanna It's the phone. When you knocked it off the hook reception must have thought you called them. Just answer it and say we're fine.

Roger You answer it. You're better at these things than me.

Joanna You want me to say, 'My husband knocked the phone over. He's an idiot'?

Roger If you like.

Joanna But it's on your side. Just pick it up!

Roger I'm trying to find it!

He picks up the receiver.

Roger Hello? Look, I'm sorry, we're fine. I'm an idio— [*beat*] Peter? Yes, Everything's OK. Nice room. We've just gone to bed and then I knocked the phone over. I thought you were … Never mind. [*beat*] What's up? Don't be daft. Really? Have you been drinking? No, that's not a good idea.

She'll be asleep by now. Just go to bed and in the morning ... Why? Where are you? All right, stay there.

Joanna What's happened? Where're you going?

Roger gets out of bed.

Roger Peter's having a bit of a queasy moment.

Joanna You mean he's ill?

Roger No. It's just the usual pre-wedding, 'Do I want to go through with this?'

Joanna The usual? Did you feel like this, before our wedd—

Roger [*cuts in*] Not now! I need to get dressed. Peter's downstairs.

Joanna You're going out? At this time of night?

Roger Yup. Where's my ...? [*exasperated*] Can you put the bloody lights on?

MUSIC BREAK

Breakfast in Bed – Dusty Springfield

SCENE 5: *Early morning, birds singing. Roger tries to creep back into the bedroom. Stumbles. falls into bed. Yawns. Joanna wakes up with a start.*

Joanna What the ...?

Roger G'night.

Joanna What time is it?

Roger I dunno. Birds singing. Sun coming up. Dawn?

Joanna Five forty-five?! You've been out all night?

Roger   Pretty much. Go back to sleep.

Joanna   No! I've slept!

Roger   Lucky you.

Joanna   Tell me what happened!

Roger   I'm too tired to speak. See you in the morning.

Light snoring from Roger.

Joanna   It *is* the morning. Wake up!

Roger   Stop shaking me!

Joanna   Is Peter all right? What did he say?

Roger   He said that when he saw the marquee he got a bit of a shock. Because it reminded him of the day he married Sally.

Joanna   That's just what we said.

Roger   And he thinks he might be making a terrible mistake, marrying Kirsty.

Joanna   Also just what we said.

Roger   *You* said.

Joanna   It can't just be the marquee. Something else must have triggered this.

Roger   Well, he was putting together the music for the reception and he discovered The Clash meant nothing to her. She wasn't even born when 'Rock the Casbah' got to number eight in the Billboard Top 100.

Joanna   I remember that summer.

Roger   So did he.

Joanna   We went to Casablanca with him and Sally so we could sing 'Rock the Casbah' in the souk.

Roger   There was quite a crowd!

Joanna   It was glorious – the colours, the smells, everybody dancing and laughing. The musicians joined in …

Roger   Yes, he talked a lot about all the things we did, the four of us. Our 'shared history', he called it.

Joanna   Well, it's obvious he won't have any shared history with someone who wasn't even born when the Spice Girls got to number one.

Roger   He got quite tearful, talking about the plans we all made for the summer, before he left Sally.

Joanna   We missed out on Latitude Festival because we didn't have his camper van. Did you remind him?

Roger   I did, actually. He didn't even smile. He was too upset.

Joanna   Do you think he still loves Sally?

Roger   In lots of ways, but he says he's very happy she's found someone. I think he's just worried about keeping up with Kirsty.

Joanna   Well, she is a fitness instructor.

Roger   But he's got a lot fitter since he's been with her.

Joanna   Has he spoken to Kirsty about how he feels?

Roger   No. Hasn't had a chance, he said. Lots of her friends have arrived, including her best mate, all the way from New York. They've been huddled together yakking away for days. He said he's not getting a look in … And she's happy. So excited.

Joanna   So Kirsty's never expressed any doubts about marrying him?

Roger   Not at all. She couldn't be more loving and

	adoring, he said. I said maybe she could give you a few tips … [*yawns*] I must get some sleep.
Joanna	Wait! So where did you do all this talking?
Roger	We met in the bar, but when they started hoovering around us we went out into the grounds.
Joanna	In the dark?
Roger	They've got low lights on the paths and then we ended up in the marquee, which was pretty depressing. Empty and cold. [*yawns*] Night.
Joanna	Just a minute! Was he really going to call the whole thing off?
Roger	Yes, I think he was seriously considering it. But we walked miles and he talked himself out of it. I mostly just listened. Now I want to *sleep*!
Joanna	You can't go to sleep in that state. Get undressed. You've got mud all over your shoes.
Roger	[*yawns*] In a minute. I just need to shut my eyes …
Joanna	What about Joe – Hermes – whatever his name is?
Roger	Well, of course he adores him, and once I'd got him talking about his life with Kirsty, he agreed it was fantastic and he was a very lucky man. To have a beautiful, young, fit, devoted wife, who never argues with him and worships the ground he … [*he trails off*] Sorry, I think I'm hallucinating …
Joanna	You didn't smoke any …?
Roger	Of course not! I'm just shattered.
Joanna	So the wedding's still on?

Roger   Very much so. He was pretty chirpy when I left him. He'll be fine.

Joanna   But will you? I'm not sure an all-nighter being an agony uncle to the groom is part of the best man's duties. Have you got to revise your speech?

Roger   It's only a couple of paragraphs anyway. I knew there was no way I could mention anything that happened more than two years ago.

Joanna   He must have been really desperate, to discuss this with you.

Roger   Thanks very much!

Joanna   You two never talk about anything but Tottenham or traffic diversions.

Roger   It did feel a bit awkward at first but he told me I'd saved his marriage, so I must have said something right.

Joanna   I'm proud of you. Well done for being a good friend. Let me give you a great big …

Roger   No! Go away! I'm tired.

Knock at the door.

Roger   Oh, God! I hope that's not Peter.

Joanna   It'll be room service. I ordered an early breakfast so we could go for a swim before the wedding.

Roger groans.

Roger   Oh, please, no! It'll be that waiter again, won't it?

Joanna   Probably. And there you are, lying on the bed, fully dressed, face down, with muddy boots on.

Roger groans again.

Roger   More fuel for the below-stairs coffee break.

Joanna Come in!
Door opens and Neville enters with breakfast tray.

MUSIC BREAK
Rock the Casbah – The Clash

SCENE 6: *Hotel lobby, early afternoon. Joanna and Roger meet.*

Roger Oh, there you are!

Joanna I've been trying to find you. How's things?

Roger [*yawns*] I'm completely shattered.

Joanna Poor darling. You must be. You've had so much to do.

Roger I'm going up to our room to have a lie-down.

Joanna I thought you still had things to sort out?

Roger I've handed everything over to Kirsty's brother.

Joanna The useless Jason?

Roger That's him. Had enough. Going to bed. Coming?

Joanna Erm … Hey! Why don't we walk around the gardens first? Clear your head?

Roger I walked round the gardens all last night.

Roger starts heading to their room, then turns.

Roger Oh, did you find Peter?

Joanna Yes. And in fact … he's shattered as well. Which is why, he's having a little sleep …

Roger Good. If anybody needs it, it's a groom who's been dumped at the altar.

Joanna … in our bed.

Roger What?!

Joanna   He's such a lost soul. He didn't know where to
         go, what to do … The hotel's still full of wedding
         guests but he didn't want to see anybody. He
         couldn't face going home and he certainly wasn't
         going up to the bridal suite.

Roger   So Peter's in our bed?

Joanna   On it, I think, rather than in it.

Roger   A fine distinction. He's invading my very personal
         space.

Joanna   That's not very nice. You can't begrudge him half
         an hour's kip, after everything he's been through
         today!

Roger   I'm not nice when I've had no sleep.

Joanna   He had no sleep last night either and he looked
         ready to drop … So I thought it was the best
         thing to do. Sorry, I should have called and told
         you but I was so busy looking after him.

Roger   You probably wouldn't have reached me. I've
         had to arrange for the wedding guests to have
         something to eat before they leave and as the
         marquee was all set up …

Joanna   They're all in the marquee, as if nothing has
         happened?

Roger   Well, not quite, but the drinks are flowing, so
         inhibitions and sensitivities are being shed and
         it's becoming as rowdy as any normal wedding
         reception. Except none of the top table are there.
         [*yawns*] I'm about to drop!

Joanna   OK. Just sit down for a minute.

She steers him towards a quiet corner.

Joanna   Here. Nobody can see us in this banquette. You could have a snooze!

Roger   Don't want to. I want my bed.

Joanna   Well, it's a big bed. I s'pose you can lie on one side of it.

Roger   Peter sleeps like a starfish. We've shared a tent. I'm not sleeping with him, that's crazy!

Joanna   I know. But it's been a crazy, crazy day, hasn't it?

Her phone pings with a text.

Joanna   Guess what. Text from Sally saying 'How did it go?' Hah! Where to begin …

Roger   How about … 'Imagine being invited to an *EastEnders* wedding'?

Joanna   [*narrating as she types out a text*] 'When the vicar said "If anyone knows any lawful impediment" and we heard "Yes! Kirsty loves *me!*" there was such a sharp intake of breath from the whole congregation, it felt like being sucked into a wind tunnel.'

Roger   He certainly knew how to make an entrance.

Joanna   Did you notice he was standing in the balcony? Just like in *The Graduate*. When Elaine's about to marry Carl and Benjamin shouts 'Elaine! Elaine'! And she runs out of the church and they jump on a bus. The end. Remember?

Roger   Yes, of course I remember, but that was a film and this is real life.

Joanna   But it's like we were at Carl and Elaine's wedding, when Mrs Robinson storms down the aisle …

Roger goes quiet.

Joanna   Are you all right?

Roger   I was just thinking … When Peter said Kirsty was
spending all her time with her best mate from
New York, I assumed it was a girl. If he'd said it
was a guy – a strapping, hunky guy her age, that
she'd known for years – I might have seen this
coming. I *should* have seen this coming.

Joanna   I don't think anybody saw it coming.

Roger   I have a feeling her parents might have done. I
saw them talking with the guy. Harry, is it? They
were directing him out of the church before she
arrived.

Joanna   You didn't tell me that!

Roger   At the time, I just thought they were showing
him where the loos were.

Joanna   Maybe they were.

Roger   One minute Peter was smiling, waiting for Kirsty,
perfectly OK, and then it all kicked off.

Joanna   It's funny, most weddings go on too long but
I've never known one that started at noon and
finished at … What time was it?

Roger   Twenty past.

Joanna   I didn't think I'd ever feel sorry for Peter until he
tried to stop Kirsty from leaving and she turned and
said, 'I can't deny the age gap any longer. It's hard to
be with a man as old as you.' He just crumpled.

Roger   Now he knows how Al Pacino felt when his

young girlfriend ditched him.

Joanna It was a low blow.

Roger In her defence, I don't think she realised she was so close to the microphone.

Joanna Don't excuse her. It was a cruel thing. She could have left him with his dignity and just said …

Roger We're musically incompatible?

Joanna Yes! Peter would have understood that. He was about to ditch her yesterday because she didn't like The Clash.

Roger On the plus side, if Harry is her age and her best friend, they'll have lots of shared musical memories.

Joanna Like S Club 7?

Roger yawns.

Joanna I would never say it to Peter but it was really romantic.

Roger Harry and Kirsty left her wedding nearly as fast as we left ours.

Joanna They even had a gorgeous car to jump into.

Roger It showed a certain bravado for him to hijack the bridal limo. He turned the chauffeur into a getaway driver.

Joanna D'you know, I think they're made for each other.

Roger Based on?

Joanna Well, they're both fast runners, for a start. Triathletes. Nobody could catch them. And Kirsty was wearing a full-length sheath dress and four-inch slingbacks!

They both laugh.

Roger I don't know why I'm laughing. It's not funny at all, is it?

Joanna But as weddings go it's the best one I've ever been to! Except ours, obviously.

Roger Come on, let's go and kick Peter out of our bed.

They walk along the corridor.

Joanna Best friends becoming lovers … What does that make you think of?

Roger Not so much *The Graduate*, more *When Harry Met Sally* – or Kirsty.

Joanna Exactly. Loved that film, too. Do you remember the scene …?

Roger I know what you're going to say and of course I remember it.

Joanna It's a little-known fact that the director Rob Reiner's mother was the lady at the next table who said, 'I'll have what she's having.'

Roger It's actually a very well-known fact.

They see Neville approaching.

Joanna Oh look, here comes your favourite person.

Roger He's smirking again. He thinks I'm some clueless, accident-prone old git.

Joanna laughs.

Joanna The evidence is stacking up …

Roger If he doesn't remove that smug expression, I'll wipe it off his face myself!

Joanna Easy, tiger! We'll get him in the end.

Roger D'you have a cunning plan?

Joanna Working on it. Meanwhile, smile! Hello, Neville.

My, you do work long hours. I wonder if you
could ask housekeeping to send some more towels
to our room? Thank you so much.

Neville walks off.

Roger Why do we want more towels?

Joanna Well, you got pretty muddy after being out all
night and then we went swimming and now
Peter's staying …

Roger He is not staying!

Joanna Shh … He might still be asleep. Have you got
your door key?

Roger Yup.

Roger opens the door. They go in.

Joanna [*quietly*] Ah … he's spark out. Bless him.

Roger Bless him, nothing! He's spread-eagled on to my
side!

Joanna Maybe I shouldn't have given him a sleeping
tablet.

Roger What?! No, maybe you damn well shouldn't! I
want my bed back!

Joanna OK. Just take your shoes off and we'll ease him
over a bit … so you can …

They move Peter back over to Joanna's side.

Joanna Now, quick! Lie down, before he rolls back!

Roger [*muffled*] Too late! I'm squashed!

Joanna Stay still!

Roger He's breathing on me! And I want him to stop
stroking my hair …

Joanna Really? It looks quite soothing.

Roger   Mmm … [*yawns*] Actually, it's not unpleasant. I
think I might be about to …

Joanna   [*in a loudish whisper*] Before you drop off, can you
just help me with this?

Roger snores, slowly and rhythmically.

Joanna   I can't undo it by myself!

Discreet knock on the door. Joanna opens it to the steward.

Joanna   Neville? I didn't expect *you* to bring the towels
personally.

Neville is staring at the bed with the two men in it.

Joanna   Ah. I see you've spotted that my husband's got his
best friend for a sleepover. I know what you're
thinking. But it is our wedding anniversary and
we always like to try something different. Ring
the changes. Will you bring another wine glass?

Neville starts to leave, hastily.

Joanna   Oh, and … Wait! Before you go, could you do
me a huge favour? Neville, would you unzip me,
please? I'd be enormously grateful. This dress is so
dreadfully tight.

Neville, shocked, departs at speed.

Joanna   Neville! Come back! Whatever's the matter?
Neville …!

*She turns back into the room in triumph and shuts the door,
laughing.*

Joanna   Got him!

Roger   Yes, I heard.

Joanna   He thought he was being invited to an oldies' orgy.

Roger   Terrifying!

Joanna   I did it for you.

Roger   I know. Thank you.

Joanna   Are you happy?

Roger   Yes, I'm very happy.

Joanna   But also very tired?

Roger   No, I feel pretty good. Let *me* unzip you.

Joanna   We can't do this with Peter asleep in the bed!

Roger   Maybe not. But there's an empty bridal suite upstairs – and Peter's got the key in his pocket.

Joanna   And it is our anniversary, sort of. Do you think Neville will be on duty upstairs?

Roger   Oh, I do hope so.

END MUSIC
Come Away with Me – Norah Jones

Just saw this - added some thoughts ...

THE JOHN I KNEW

John was younger, fitter and cleverer than me so I certainly never expected to be doing this today. I'm still numb with shock that my wonderful, warm, oldest friend has left us so suddenly. But if I feel angry and bereft I can only imagine the heartbreak of Marion and his family.

Nice start. In tears already

Mention Calum, Rosie and John's sister, Joan ...

Marion's sister is Jane, not Joan! You've known her for forty years! And don't forget Rosie is pregnant so he was about to become a grandfather again

The university years - John's leadership in everything from rugby to debates. Memories Boating/ Accidents/ Climbing up the ivy/ season ticket at A&E ...

Remember to say he met Marion on the river. Crashed into her boat and then rescued her!

John was way above me in every kind of achievement but one thing we had in common was that we each chose our life partner wisely and well. A long and happy marriage is the greatest joy in life and probably, John would say, his proudest achievement. Which is why we will be there for Marion in the days and months ahead, offering help, sharing memories and missing John together.

In tears again. Well done! Love you xxx

If You Go Away

SCENE 1: *Day one. Joanna and Roger have been out for lunch and she has had some chest pains. They are driving to the hospital.*

Joanna Oh, let's just go back home.

Roger No. We're going to the hospital. Get you checked out.

Joanna Remember when I bandaged up your hand when you cut it with the kitchen knife? And it was fine.

Roger This isn't a knife cut.

Joanna I know, but this'll probably pass. And hospitals have got far more important things to worry about …

Roger Nearly there.

Joanna I'm frightened.

Roger I know.

Joanna Say something.

Roger If I say, 'It'll be fine', you'll say, 'You don't know that!' And if I say, 'Of course you're frightened. It could be serious', you'll say, 'That's not helpful.

	Stop scaring me.' Normally, I'd put my arm round you, because that is usually the safest option, but I can't do that because I'm driving.
Joanna	That's a very analytical response to an emergency.
Roger	Proves my point. I can't win. But whatever it is, we'll deal with it together, OK?
Joanna	My phone battery's low.
Roger	Want me to go back and get your charger?
Joanna	Erm …
Roger	That was a joke!
Joanna	I don't want you to make jokes.
Roger	I'm sorry. Does it still hurt?
Joanna	Yes. Right across my chest. A kind of tightness, like a too-small bra. Only worse. And also, a fluttery feeling. I can hear my heart in my ears.
Roger	OK. Try and breathe slowly …
Joanna	I don't want to die!
Roger	You won't die.
Joanna	You don't know that. You're not a doctor.
Roger	But trust me, I'm a husband.
Joanna	My dad was only sixty-two when he died –
Roger	I know.
Joanna	– of a heart attack.
Roger	I remember. Very sudden.
Joanna	He had chest pains. Took some aspirin. Didn't think anything of it.
Roger	Typical of his generation … Stoic.
Joanna	And then he just died. Younger than I am now. It was a huge shock.

Roger   It was. I was there.

Joanna   And I had chest pains for months afterwards.

Roger   Psychosomatic. You were told that.

Joanna   But I've got his genes.

Roger   More importantly, you've also got your mother's genes and if she hadn't broken her hip playing tennis at ninety-six, she'd still be with us.

Joanna   I never have anything wrong with me, do I?

Roger   No. You're a superwoman.

Joanna   I haven't got time to be ill. I've got the reunion this week. I can't let the girls down.

Roger   You don't know that you're ill. We've just had a long lunch …

Joanna   You think it could be indigestion?

Roger   Seems a distinct possibility.

Joanna   I don't get indigestion. You're the one who takes a bucketload of Rennies after a mild curry. Not me. I can eat anything.

Roger   I discovered that the night we met. You pinched my chips.

Joanna   You offered me one!

Roger   But you took six. Of the biggest. That's when I knew you were the one for me.

Joanna   Interesting criteria.

Roger   A woman who loves food usually has a very healthy appetite in other areas.

Joanna laughs, cautiously.

Roger   And so it proved.

Joanna   Don't make me laugh. It really hurts now.

Roger Sorry, darling. Take some deep breaths. Here we are. I'll drop you at A&E and park the car.

Joanna No. I don't want to go in on my own. I want you with me.

Roger OK. Well, I'll have to try and find a space first …

Roger's window winds down as they go through the car-park entrance. A small plastic token drops down and he retrieves it.

Roger Hang on to this stupid token for a sec …

Joanna Tell me something else about us.

Roger What? I'm trying to park!

Joanna I know, but … I'd like to have something to think about, while I'm … in there. Having tests. Maybe a heart operation …

Roger I love you. Will that do? Now, keep your eyes peeled.

Roger circles the car park, trying to find a space.

Joanna It's busy, isn't it? Visiting time, of course. I'll make a wish to the Parking Fairy.

Roger What's that Skoda doing? Is he leaving?

Joanna No, he's on his phone. What do you love about me?

Roger That you never give up trying to turn me into the man you deserve.

Joanna [*sounding satisfied*] And I'm almost there. Just got to prise you away from your twenty-four-hour TV news addiction …

Roger Look, if I can't find a space soon, you'll just have to get out.

Joanna Oh look, it worked! She's leaving, in the Mini.

Roger   Yes!

Joanna   Thank you, Parking Fairy!

They park. Roger gets out, comes round and opens Joanna's door.

Roger   OK. Come on. Take my hand.

Joanna is still in her seat, scared.

Joanna   I don't want to go in there. I want to stay with
you. I'm scared about what they'll say when they
see me.

Roger   They'll say, 'Who's the lucky guy with that
beautiful woman?'

Joanna   I love you. Did I say that? Oh, I'd better give you
the car-park token, in case …

Roger   Keep it. We'll be coming home together.

MUSIC BREAK

Have I Told You Lately – Van Morrison

SCENE 2: *Joanna and Roger's house, two hours later. The key
turns in the door and they both walk in.*

Joanna   Oh, hello, gorgeous house! Hello, lovely, lovely
coat stand! Hello, divine Art Deco mirror! Hello,
me! I look happy! I *am* happy!

Roger laughs.

Roger   You hide it so well.

Joanna   And thank you, darling. Let me give you a great
big kiss!

She kisses Roger.

Roger   Woah! You've been told to avoid excitement.

Joanna   I'm definitely giving up coffee.

Roger   Good idea. But I think it was the fact that it was Turkish coffee – and you had three cups of it.

Joanna   I should have known. We mostly have decaff these days. Not used to it. But I love my one cup of proper coffee in the morning. Do you think I should give that up, too?

Roger   Did they give you specific advice?

Joanna   They asked me a lot of daft questions. Like can I cut my own toenails! Jeepers!

Roger   That's not a daft question. Given your age.

Joanna   I think we all know it's not when you were born but your biological age that counts.

Roger   Yes, but they don't know you're an age-defying wonderwoman, often mistaken for my daughter. All they had was your birth date. Did they actually tell you to give up caffeine?

Joanna   I told you. They said the excess caffeine had made my heart race but I had an ECG and they said there was no evidence I'd had an 'incident' as they called it.

Roger   Your blood pressure was a bit high, though.

Joanna   Yes. But I was very stressed.

Roger   Did they suggest you go on statins?

Joanna   Sort of.

Roger   That means yes.

Joanna   They want everybody to go on statins.

Roger   For a reason. Did you agree?

Joanna   I just said let me see if I can fix it myself first.

Roger   You're not Marie Curie.

Joanna   But I want to be in charge of my own health.

Roger   Look, I know you're very fit and do a lot of exercise, but we're both getting older …

Joanna starts humming.

Roger   Stop humming and listen.

Joanna   Don't want to listen.

Roger   Take your fingers out of your ears. This time it was probably just a caffeine overdose –

Joanna   It *was*!

Roger   – and I know you think you're immortal –

Joanna   I don't. I just know my own body and I want to look after it my way – preferably without pills.

Roger   – but although you're not on any medication at the moment, don't dismiss the possibility that there might come a time when there's something you can't fix with Pilates, swimming or a bolshie attitude.

Joanna   I'm not being bolshie. I'm going to get a blood pressure monitor machine and keep a record and see our doctor in a month. Who is our doctor?

Roger   I think it's about time you found out.

Joanna   Stop lecturing me.

Roger   I'm not, but …

Joanna   I have regular check-ups, annual blood tests. I don't smoke. Any more.

Roger   I agree, you're doing all the right things …

Joanna   Would you rather I was a delicate little flower who had a fit of the vapours every time she lifted

a roast chicken out of the oven, or rushed to the
doctors with a splinter?

Roger   Well, at least I'd be able to protect somebody like
that.

Joanna   I don't need protection.

Roger   That's my point. If you won't let me look after
you, I want to be sure you're looking after
yourself, because without you, my life would be a
lot less ... noisy.

Joanna laughs.

Joanna   OK. I promise I'll look after myself. Coffee?

Roger   That didn't last long.

MUSIC BREAK
Black Coffee in Bed – Squeeze

SCENE 3: *Roger and Joanna's bedroom, later that night. Joanna
is sobbing.*

Roger   Hey, what's the matter? What time is it?

Joanna   Three forty-seven.. No, three forty-eight.

Roger   What's up?

Joanna   Do you think we'll ever go back to Australia?

Roger   Ermm ... Do you want to?

Joanna   I liked it a lot.

Roger   Me too.

Joanna   Sad not to see it again.

Roger   There's no reason why we won't see it again, if it's
that important to you.

Joanna	Marion and John are going. They've been lots of times.
Roger	They've got grandchildren in Melbourne.
Joanna	We haven't.
Roger	I know!
Joanna	We've never been to Machu Picchu.
Roger	True.
Joanna	Or the Galapagos.
Roger	Because you said that both those places had been overrun with tourists and we shouldn't add to the hordes that were destroying them.
Joanna	Did I?
Roger	Yes. Quite often.
Joanna	Time's running out, you said.
Roger	When?
Joanna	You said we're getting older.
Roger	You were humming. You didn't hear that.
Joanna	I did. And it's true.
Roger	Everyone is getting older. Oh, I know what this is about.
Joanna	Do you? I don't.
Roger	You got very scared today … yesterday … when you thought you might be having a heart attack and then you got very euphoric when you realised you weren't going to die and now, in the empty hours of the night, you're getting a reaction to all this.
Joanna	Did you know HS2 won't be finished till at least twenty forty?

Roger   [*confused*] Oh, ye gods! What the …? Yes, I did. So?

Joanna   It's twenty years away! That's so upsetting.

Roger   Only if you need to get to Leeds or Manchester in a belting hurry – and I don't think you ever have.

Joanna   That's not the point.

Roger   It's not?

Joanna   The point is, we may not be … *around* by the time it's finished.

Roger   Judging by its progress so far, I think the same might be true of today's teenagers.

Joanna   We could be dead by twenty forty!

Roger   So you're upset because we might die before the train line's completed?

Joanna   I'm upset because we might die!

Roger   There's no 'might' about it.

Joanna   I don't want to be in a world if we're not in it, do you?

Roger   The chances of finding a remotely sane answer to that question are slim to impossible.

Joanna   We can't go yet!

Roger   We're *not* going yet!

Joanna   What have we achieved? What is our legacy?

Roger   We worked hard, made lots of friends, and, mostly, we were kind.

Joanna   But there'll be no blue plaques outside our house. I want a blue plaque. I'd like to have one that says secret agent, like Violette Szabo.

Roger   You're too young to have been a secret agent.

Joanna   Or Virginia McKenna! She saved animals.

Roger   We've saved a few. The rabbit who got caught in the fence. And the hedgehog who nearly drowned in the pond. And we saved Bonzo Dog's life a few times – adder bite, and when he swallowed the squeaker from his bunny.

Joanna   But we're not in *Who's Who*. No one will say, 'Oh, he played cricket for England', or, 'She campaigned for human rights'.

Roger   You went to Greenham Common.

Joanna   Everyone did that.

Roger   And we both marched against the war in Vietnam.

Joanna   That didn't mark us out as exceptional. Everyone we knew did those things.

Roger   And you organised the community care during lockdown.

Joanna   [*grumbling*] But they wouldn't let me deliver shopping or anything because I was in the 'vulnerable age group' myself.

Roger   I'm glad I didn't have to tell you that. But you manned the phone lines.

Joanna   That's not going to get me a damehood. No one will talk about us when we're gone.

Roger   Our friends will.

Joanna   They'll all be gone, too! And we have no children. We'll be forgotten.

Roger   We have godchildren.

Joanna   It's not the same. We haven't created a dynasty!

Roger   We're not the House of Windsor.

Joanna   We thought we could change the world.

Roger   We jolly well did change a lot of the world. And
our generation is still changing it. Or trying to.

Joanna   I want an obituary in *The Times*.

Roger   Saying what?

Joanna   She won The Booker Prize?

Roger   You have to write a book first.

Joanna   Or rode a motorcycle round the Wall of Death.
Anything! Recognition that I was here. I was
alive.

Roger   But you won't be there to read it.

Joanna   I know! That's what's so sad.

MUSIC BREAK

If You Go Away – Scott Walker

SCENE 4: *The kitchen, the next morning. Roger is doing the
crossword at the table. Joanna enters, frantic. Roger is absorbed in
the paper.*

Joanna   It's John!

Roger   Great! Bring him in. I need help with this
crossword.

Joanna   He's gone!

Roger   That was bloody quick! Is he off to the airport?

Joanna   No, he's really gone. He's dead! John has died! In
the departure lounge!

Roger   Oh, my God! How? What happened?

Joanna   Rosie just phoned. He collapsed. They tried CPR

	but … I can't believe it.
Roger	We only saw them in The Grapes last week.
Joanna	Such a happy, fun evening. He was talking about doing the Marathon.
Roger	I'll call Marion. See if she needs help.
Joanna	I asked Rosie that but she said, 'It's OK. I'm bringing Mum back and I'm staying.' I told her we'd go round tonight. I'll take her something to eat. Not that she'll be hungry.
Roger	John. Of all people. Superfit cyclist, runner, brain the size of a planet …
Joanna	All round genuinely lovely guy. Marion's terribly upset.
Roger	Well, naturally. They've been together nearly as long as us.
Joanna	Yes, but she's even more distressed because they had a row, Rosie said. The flight was just called and Marion realised she hadn't got any antihistamine, so she said she'd nip to the chemist and John said, 'We're not going to the Mongolian salt plains! You can get some in Australia.' And she said, 'I might need them on the flight' – you know she's got lots of allergies – and he got really, really cross …
Roger	That's not like John. I've never seen John lose his temper. Maybe he's scared of flying?
Joanna	No. He's flown all over the world. Anyway, Marion stormed off and when she came back, he was on the floor, surrounded by people.
Roger	God, that's really terrible.

Joanna   Rosie said she's inconsolable.

Roger   I'm not surprised.

Joanna   Because she thinks it's her fault he collapsed.

Roger   Bound to. That'll take her a while to come to terms with.

Joanna   You know what he said to her? 'Bugger off to Boots, then. But I might be gone when you get back.' He just meant the queue might move forward!

Roger   Of course he did.

Joanna   But those were the last words he ever said to her. 'I might be gone when you get back.'

Roger   That's really hard.

Joanna   He was cross with her when he died! How heartbreaking is that?

Roger   And she was buzzing around Boots, probably calling him names …

Joanna   And also, she wasn't with him when he died. Just strangers …

Roger   More guilt for her.

Joanna   He should be in Australia, laughing with the grandchildren.

Roger   And instead, Marion's planning his funeral.

Joanna   Who would have ever thought John would go first? Marion's the one with the chronic conditions – asthma and diabetes. Bloody death! Taking really good people, who are so loved … It's not fair.

Roger   Death isn't fair. Just inevitable.

Joanna Yes, at the end of a long, long life, but John …
He loved life! So much. I was talking to someone
last week about how lucky we were that we
hadn't lost anyone we loved and – oh, God, it was
Marion! I was talking to Marion, in the pub. She
was saying she was a bit apprehensive about flying
to Oz but she had to weigh that against them not
seeing the grandchildren. And now he won't.

Roger And we'll never see him again. An appalling loss.

Joanna We seem to be going to more funerals than
weddings these days.

Roger That's just the age we are.

Joanna Do you think about dying every day?

Roger Not every day any more.

Joanna I really thought I was going to die yesterday! I
thought my heart would just stop.

Roger I know. And I could go tomorrow.

Joanna Don't say that. Give me a big hug.

Roger OK. But I am planning to still be here tomorrow.

Joanna Have you fixed the gate?

Roger What?!

Joanna I don't know why I thought of that.

Roger [*sighs*] I do.

MUSIC BREAK

Sometimes We Cry – Van Morrison

SCENE 5: *Roger and Joanna are walking in the park.*

Joanna   It's good to get some fresh air, isn't it?

Roger   Wonderful. But as you seem to be pacesetting for a middle-distance runner, I think my knee could do with a rest. Shall we sit down here for a bit? If we can avoid the bird crap.

They sit.

Joanna   It must be great being a pigeon.

Roger   Pass.

Joanna   Or any bird. Because it's a sure thing that being high on a hill on a clear day will ease your mind.

Roger   Like a bridge over troubled water?

Joanna   All those people down there in the streets. Some of them are lonely, or sick, or have lost someone …

Roger   And others are deliriously happy, celebrating good news or planning a wedding.

Joanna   Don't tell me to cheer up.

Roger   I wouldn't dare.

Joanna   I heard you get up in the night again.

Roger   Neither of us are sleeping very well, are we? Not surprising.

Joanna   I keep thinking about poor Marion.

Roger   Me too – and how I'm going to write this eulogy.

Joanna   Has Marion decided whether to say something?

Roger   There's no way she can do it. She's just sent me the quote she was talking about.

Joanna   The Shakespearean one?

Roger   Yup. She wants me to say it at the end, on her behalf.

Joanna   Which one is it?

Roger   I've got it on my phone. Do you want to hear it?

Joanna   Will it make me cry again?

Roger   Undoubtedly.

Joanna   Read it to me, then. Wait! Let me find a tissue first … OK. Go on.

Roger   'Come, gentle night, come, loving, black-brow'd night, Give me my Romeo; and, when he shall die, Take him and cut him out in little stars, And he will make the face of heaven so fine that all the world will be in love with night.'

Silence.

Roger   Are you all right?

Joanna   [*tearful*] How are you going to read that out with Marion sitting in front of you?

Roger   I'm going to do it flawlessly, because she trusts me. She's given me this huge responsibility and it's an honour. The one thing that I can do for our friend, John.

Joanna   You're too good for me.

Roger   Yes, I am. But I like having you around because you make me feel superior.

Joanna laughs.

Joanna   I'd forgotten how to laugh!

Roger   Don't ever do that.

Joanna   How're you going to sum up John in fifteen minutes?

Roger   That's what's keeping me awake at night.

Joanna   He should have a blue plaque, shouldn't he?
International peacekeeper, lots of gongs and
honours. Half-page obit in *The Times*.

Roger   I loved the line about 'His matchless
communication skills were never put to better use
than in his nurturing of lifelong friendships'. I'm
going to use that.

Joanna   Will you run it past Marion first?

Roger   Not sure. What do you think?

Joanna   On the plus side, she'll know what's coming.

Roger   On the minus side, she's trying to keep it together
till the funeral. I don't want to upset her even
more.

Joanna   She's a tough cookie but this will be the worst
day of her life.

Roger   I'll only show it to her if she asks me.

Joanna   Strange things, eulogies. When you say all the
things you should have said to them when they
were alive.

Roger   But didn't.

Joanna   I think we should write each other's eulogies.

Roger   I don't need to write yours because you told me I
was going to go first.

Joanna   That was before my health scare.

Roger   You didn't have a health scare, you had too much
coffee.

Joanna   But look at John. He was incredibly fit. And he
went like that. We need to be prepared.

Roger	I'm always prepared. I was a Queen's Scout.
Joanna	But if somebody dies, you're in no fit state to compose your thoughts and memories. You should have it ready. So, shall we do that?
Roger	What?
Joanna	Write each other's eulogies? Before we have to.
Roger	Let me get this one done first.
Joanna	Then will you write my eulogy?
Roger	Why?!
Joanna	I just said why.
Roger	Yes, but that's not the truth, is it? You just want to know what I am going to say about you.
Joanna	Of course I do!
Roger	Most partners find it impossible to stand up and talk about their other half. Eulogies are often delivered by friends. Like this one.
Joanna	I don't want my friends to deliver my eulogy.
Roger	Why not? Diana or Sally could do it – or Jacky has known you from schooldays.
Joanna	Oh, God, no!
Roger	Is that such a bad idea?
Joanna	Jacky! I forgot. The reunion is the same day as the funeral, isn't it?
Roger	You could still go. The funeral won't last into the evening.
Joanna	No, I can't. It's at Jacky's place. I'd have to stay overnight.
Roger	You can get together some other time.
Joanna	But this is special. We couldn't do it last year,

217

obviously, so now it's fifty-six years since we left the sixth form. She's worked so hard at organising this and getting us all together.

Roger She'll understand.

Joanna Remind me to call her the minute we get home.

Roger Tell her if you're not there, she can write your eulogy. Absent friends.

Joanna No. I want you to write my eulogy. What would you say about me?

Roger How do I love thee, let me count the ways?

Joanna Seriously. I want to be sure you'll say nice things.

Roger Why don't you write it, then?

Joanna Write my own eulogy? That seems like …

Roger A really good idea?

Joanna Well, it does but … No, I can't do that.

Roger Why not?

Joanna It's what other people think about you. Not what you think about yourself.

Roger Yes, but who's gonna know? I won't tell them. You can write your own eulogy and what you want me to say and I'll just change the personal pronouns. Sorted. Don't know why I didn't think of that sooner. And hey, that could work for your birthday and anniversary cards, too! You write the message you'd like to read and I'll copy it out. Oh, hang on! Also, you find the card that you like, so I won't have to spend endless hours debating whether to get you a soulful Labrador or a high-kicking flapper and have to watch your face fall

with disappointment as you open it and I realise,
once again, I've made the wrong choice.

Joanna   That wouldn't work.

Roger   It would for me.

Joanna   But I want to know what *you* really think about
me and how *you'll* remember me.

Roger   OK, but you start. What would *you* say about *me*?

Joanna   I'd say … [*she thinks for a moment*] you're the
one I couldn't wait to see, if we'd been apart.
Even if I'd only been swimming, or at work,
or at my mother's, I'd get so excited that I was
coming home to you. I'd stop the car up the
road and touch up my lipstick and have a quick
squirt of Estée Lauder – maybe I'd only been
to Waitrose for meatballs – but I would rush in
and—

Roger   [*cuts in*] Let me stop you right there.

Joanna   Why?

Roger   Because this is my eulogy you're writing and
it seems to be all about you. In the car … in
Waitrose … at your mother's …

Joanna   It's about the effect you have on me.

Roger   Nah. Vanity project.

Joanna   That's not fair!

Roger   Please don't start crying.

Joanna   Remember when you bought me Lillian
Hellman's book, *Pentimento*?

Roger   No.

Joanna   Well, all right. I bought it for my birthday for you to give to me. And you wrapped it up – once I found you some wrapping paper …

Roger   Oh, yes. Got it now. What about it?

Joanna   She wrote about her life with Dashiell Hammett. They'd been together for twenty years –

Roger   Lightweights.

Joanna   – some of them bad, a few of them shabby …

Roger   Much like us.

Joanna   Exactly. But she couldn't wait to talk to him. To hear what he thought about the news, a departing guest, a walk in the woods. Their relationship survived for the strongest of reasons, their pleasure in each other. They were living the best of times together, she said.

Roger   Wasn't he a violent, promiscuous drunk?

Joanna   Sometimes …

Roger   And she was famous for being economical with the truth, as I recall …?

Joanna   I never said they were perfect.

Roger   You think we're like them?

Joanna   I know they were flawed but they had passion for each other and I thought, that's how I feel about you. It's the physical presence of someone who is totally on your side, waiting for you, looking out for you. Marion was telling me yesterday that she walked into the kitchen thinking, 'I must tell John this,' and then came the icy shock that he would never be there to hear anything she said again. It's losing the togetherness of a good marriage, and I

can see why she chose Juliet's speech because she
wants him still to be there, somewhere, in the stars
… [*brisk*] But that's not the sort of thing I'd tell
you over breakfast, so I'll put it in your eulogy.

Roger   When I won't be there to hear it?

Joanna   I've given you a preview. Wanna know how it
ends?

Roger   There's more?

Joanna   Yes. So I shoosh up my hair and run through the
door, looking for you, wanting to share my news
with you, and you've got your head under the car
bonnet or you're watching the cricket and you
don't even look up!

Roger   That'll get a laugh – and that's a rare thing at a
funeral.

Joanna   Why are you looking over there?

Roger   Thought that dog looked a bit like Bonzo.

Joanna   It doesn't look at all like Bonzo. Are you crying?

Roger   No.

Joanna   Don't cry.

Roger   [*crying*] I'm not crying.

Joanna   You are. I'm glad you're crying.

Roger   Are you?

Joanna   Yes. Let it all out. It's John, isn't it?

Roger   No. Well, it is a bit. But mostly … It's you.

MUSIC BREAK
Sunshine of Your Love – Cream

SCENE 6: *Roger and Joanna's house. They've been back from the funeral for an hour or so. Roger has fallen asleep in his armchair and the news is just ending on TV.*

Newscaster V/O And that's all the news for now, so over to Helen at the weather centre. Good evening.

Joanna enters with a yawning sigh. Roger wakes with a start.

Roger Oh! Must have dropped off! Shattered.

Joanna Not surprised. Grieving is very tiring, isn't it? But your eulogy was perfect.

She gets a bit tearful.

Roger One of the toughest things I've ever done. So many stories. Right back to the time he nearly drowned me in the River Cam, trying to turn a punt round.

Joanna Everybody loved the one about you trying to teach him the paso doble for his wedding dance with Marion.

Roger He had three left feet.

Joanna It's been an emotional day.

Roger It has. Have you finished the Reunion Zoom call?

Joanna Yes. Have you got a tissue?

Roger Here.

He hands her a tissue. She blows her nose.

Roger Still thinking about the funeral?

Joanna No. It's just the girls ...

Roger But I thought I could hear you laughing?

Joanna Yes, it was lovely.

Roger So those are happy tears, are they?

Joanna	Of course they are. After all the sad tears we've cried today, it makes a change, doesn't it?
Roger	So. Tell me how it went. Did everyone have a dirty martini, as instructed?
Joanna	Yes. Not their first … Except for Dizzy and Tubs.
Roger	Sounds like a seventies cop show.
Joanna	Coincidentally, they're both on antibiotics for cystitis and—
Roger	[*cuts in*] Just give me the highlights. What did you talk about?
Joanna	Literature, art, politics, comparative religions …
Roger	Don't believe you.
Joanna	OK. We talked about why eyebrows go grey, the importance of tightening the pelvic floor and whether coral nail varnish looks a bit cheap in the winter.
Roger	Girl stuff.
Joanna	Also, we talked about patronising husbands.
Roger	Do you know any?
Joanna	It was all very good fun.
Roger	So what made you cry?
Joanna	Because … When I phoned Jacky the other day to tell her why I couldn't come to the reunion, I said we'd been talking about friends writing our eulogy and you said you thought she could do mine.
Roger	And you said 'No chance'.
Joanna	Yes. And she laughed but then she said it got her thinking. Usually, we sit around when we get

223

together and come up with the odd anecdote, but she put everyone's name in a hat and whoever's name they drew out, they had to do a one-minute presentation on what that girl was like at school.

Roger   Brilliant idea. Pity you weren't there.

Joanna   Well, I was. Sort of. I couldn't do one – but Jacky talked about me. On Zoom, just now.

Roger   And she didn't warn you?

Joanna   No. The girls were all in on it and they'd torn each other to pieces earlier, according to Tubs, so I didn't know what to expect.

Roger   Is that why you came down for another drink?

Joanna   Yes. And it wasn't enough.

Roger   Oh, dear.

Joanna   Jacky talked about all the detentions and how I was caught with the gardener's son in the tool shed –

Roger   Appropriate.

Joanna   – and got banned from games. Which was unfortunate, as I was Games Captain.

Roger   And still are, in so many ways.

Joanna   And then she said that there was no one she'd rather have on her side.

Roger   Are we talking about hockey or netball?

Joanna   Cos when she was being bullied by the terrible twins, June and Marcia, and they gave her a Chinese burn and stole her dinner money, I went and got it back for her, which anybody could have done, because the twins were really cowards.

Roger   Did you take a hockey stick?

Joanna   Course not. A lacrosse stick is much more subtle.
I'd forgotten all about it.

Roger   Was that when you came down for the third drink?

Joanna   Uh-huh! Anyway, she said a lot of really, really
nice things and then …

Her eyes well up.

Roger   And then what? She said something nasty?

Joanna   No, not at all. She said that they decided to take
a vote round the supper table earlier on who was
the most popular girl in school.

She gulps down a sob.

Roger   And it wasn't you? It's OK. Still love you.

Joanna   It was me! She said everyone wanted to be my
friend and the younger ones had crushes on
me. And I also had the shortest miniskirt! And I
haven't changed a bit, they said, and they all raised
a glass! To me!

Roger   Wow! That's some eulogy!

Joanna   It's not a eulogy.

Roger   Yes, it is. We've hijacked the word for funeral
speeches but it just means words of praise. And
they were. So. Most Popular Girl? Is there a cash
prize to go with it?

Joanna   Sadly, no. But it made me very happy.

Roger   Me too. And very proud.

Joanna   You had nothing to do with it.

Roger   I'm proud that I won the heart of the most
popular girl in school.

MUSIC BREAK

MUSIC BREAK

(Remember the Days of the) Old Schoolyard – Cat Stevens

SCENE 7: *A few weeks later. Roger is in the front garden. Joanna comes through the gate. Gate shuts.*

Roger   Oh, hi!

Joanna   You fixed the gate!

Roger   Yup. It 'swings like a pendulum do'.

Joanna   The garage door's still a bit wonky.

Roger   Let me just bask in the glory of one job well done. How was Marion?

Joanna   Almost serene. I asked her if she was taking anything. She said 'wine'. But it's really going to hit her when Calum goes back to Australia next week.

Roger   She could go with him.

Joanna   She could – but it's too soon. Still, he's dealt with everything and sorted out lots of stuff and he said, 'I know Mum's friends will look after her.'

Roger   Of course we will. I can do some odd jobs.

Joanna   When you've finished our odd jobs!

Roger   Look, I've dug out my old tool belt, for when I'm on the move.

Joanna   Steady! You'll be giving Bob the Builder sleepless nights.

Roger   I know you like the look of a man who knows his spanners from his mole wrench.

Joanna   I'm finding it hard to control myself.

226

Roger   It's even got a pouch for the WD40. I'll go and give the gate a squirt …

Joanna heads for the front door.

Joanna   I'll just get changed and then I'll sweep up this sawdust.

Roger   I'll do that! Stop!

Joanna   Why?

Roger   There's something at the door.

Joanna   Something? What does that mean?

Roger   It means what it says. By the door, there is something.

Joanna   Yes, me.

Roger   Apart from you. Well, not apart from you, actually … Because of you.

Joanna   You're not making any sense.

Roger   Look! At the door!

Joanna   I'm looking at the door. Same old door. Scuff marks …

Roger   OK. Widen your search! Look round the door.

Joanna   You mean behind it?

Roger   No, I bloody don't!

Joanna   All right, don't get ratty!

Roger   Was ever a surprise harder to spring?

Joanna   A surpr— Oh! Is this a blue plaque?

Roger   At last! Yes, it is!

Joanna   On the wall. We've got a blue plaque!

Roger   I know.

Joanna   Who put it there?

Roger   Me!

Joanna So somebody important lived here?

Roger Yes.

Joanna Well done for finding out! Who was it?

Roger Put your glasses on.

Joanna Just tell me.

Roger No. Read it yourself.

Joanna Oh, God, you're so tetchy.

Roger Sorry. Well?

Joanna [*reads*] 'The Most Popular Girl in School lives here with a very lucky man.' [*she laughs*] Oh, that's absolutely wonderful, darling! And I'm a very lucky woman.

Roger You are.

Joanna Thank you.

Roger Well, you said you wanted a blue plaque.

Joanna I also said I wanted a Lamborghini. Is it in the garage?

Roger Is there no pleasing this woman?

Joanna You have pleased me. It's an amazing thing to do. Did you have any help?

Roger If you mean did I have to consult your friends for advice, no. It was all me.

Joanna Even more impressed.

Roger Does it make up for the Dyson I bought you for our anniversary?

Joanna Still a way to go but it's a big step in the right direction. Let me give you a hug.

Roger It's worth more than a hug.

Joanna It'll have to do for now. We're in the street.

They hug.

Joanna Ooooh, what's that?

Roger You're squashing my measuring tape.

Joanna laughs.

Roger Did you say you were caught with the gardener's son in the tool shed?

Joanna Yes, I was.

Roger We have a tool shed. Round the back.

Joanna I know, but I don't want to get banned from games again.

Roger Let's risk it ...

They laugh.

END MUSIC

Have I Told You Lately? – Van Morrison

Gone shopping. This is what I'm cooking tonight.
No substitutions!

Crevettes with samphire, Pasta puttanesca,
Baked peaches and Crème fraiche ...

Followed by SEX!! Keep everything on a low simmer
till I'm back from Pilates, darling! xxx

I've Been Loving You Too Long
To Stop Now

OPENING MUSIC
The Things We Do for Love — 10cc

SCENE 1: *Mid evening. Joanna and Roger are watching TV. The programme is just ending.*

Roger That wasn't very good, was it?

Joanna How do you know? You nodded off ten minutes ago.

Roger I was listening with my eyes closed.

Joanna It's called sleeping.

Roger Well, I'm fully rested now. So what's on next?

Joanna What do you want to watch?

Roger Tell me what you fancy.

Joanna I asked you first.

Roger I only want to watch what makes you happy.

Joanna But I'm not fussed. Just pick something.

Roger OK. Let's see what's on and make an informed choice.

Joanna You've got the TV section.

Roger I haven't.

Joanna You're lying on it.

Roger Oh, right. What day is it?

Joanna Wednesday. I think.

Roger Do you fancy a drama? A comedy? A documentary?

Joanna Just choose anything and that'll be fine by me!

Roger You say that but if I said we should watch … erm … what's this? *A History of Ancient Britain: The Priests of Orkney* …

Joanna I'd be cock-a-hoop!

Roger Baloney! You'd rugby tackle the remote out of my clenched fist and switch over to *Strictly Come Bake Off*.

Joanna I'm sure they were fascinating people.

Roger The ancient British priests of Orkney?

Joanna Yes. Let's find out. Give me the remote.

Roger Get off! I don't want to watch that. How about Louis Theroux in San Quentin prison?

Joanna Seen it.

Roger *Nightmare Neighbour Next Door*? *Football's Funniest Moments*? *Filthy Britain SOS*?

Joanna Is there anything that requires more than one brain cell?

Roger There's a film – *Meet the Parents*.

Joanna Already met them. We saw it on a plane.

Roger *The Planets*. With Brian Cox. Jupiter The Joybringer!

Joanna That's great but so hypnotic, it sends me to sleep.

Roger Jupiter didn't bring much joy to the rest of the solar system.

Joanna   You don't say.

Roger   Bit of a bully. Shoved other planets out of the way.
I could tell you a lot about its path of destruction.

Joanna yawns.

Joanna   Please don't.

Roger   Am I boring you?

Joanna   Quite a bit, yes.

Roger   You can also be boring at times.

Joanna   Can I?

Roger   Rampaging on about traffic wardens and
processed cheese …

Joanna   Well, obviously a lovely cheese does not thrive
sealed in plastic packaging!

Roger   And she's off!

Joanna   Do you think we're a boring couple?

Roger   Everyone argues over what to watch on TV.

Joanna   I'm not talking about that. It's just … We're in a
bit of a rut, don't you think?

Roger   No, I don't.

Joanna   We don't seem to do very much. We're indoors
watching TV almost every night.

Roger   Like most people.

Joanna   Who are also stuck in a rut!

Roger   I don't mind a rut. I find a rut quite comforting
and if I had to be in a rut with anyone, I'd be
happy to be in a rut with you.

Joanna   That's nice. But unhelpful.

Roger is grazing through the TV pages.

Roger   Got it! When in doubt: *Game of Thrones*!

Joanna   No! Absolutely not! Anyway, you've seen them all.

Roger   *Das Boot?*

Joanna   I'm too tired for subtitles.

Roger   *Gomorrah?*

Joanna   That's horrible and bloody.

Roger   I like horrible and bloody.

Joanna   We're not watching it.

Roger   Even though I want to?

Joanna   But I don't.

Roger   I never stop you watching *Grand Designs.*

Joanna   You just come in every five minutes and say,
         'Haven't they got the roof on yet?'

Roger   Let's find something we both like, then.

Joanna   There's no such thing. We're TV incompatible.

Roger   Must be a programme somewhere we can agree
         on.

Joanna   But we never find it because we get cross-eyed
         trawling through hundreds of choices and give up.

Roger   There's a few boxsets we haven't finished.

Joanna   There's a few boxsets you don't remember
         finishing. You never saw the end of *Normal People.*

Roger   [*dismissively*] Didn't want to. It was rude.

Joanna   You are so Mary Whitehouse!

Roger   A fine woman. With strong values. She wouldn't
         have liked it.

Joanna   But there's lots of sex in *Game of Thrones* and you
         like that.

Roger   That's different. It's not soppy sex.

Joanna   *Normal People* wasn't soppy. It was beautiful.

Roger   It was soft porn.

Joanna   They were young and in love.

Roger   And bonking by numbers.

Joanna   Exploring each other's bodies!

Roger   Exploring? More like excavating.

Joanna   It reminded me of our early years.

Roger   It reminded me of looking for a lost biro.
Whenever the story got going, they took their kit off and had a rummage around every nook and cranny.

Joanna   That was to illustrate their obsession with each other.

Roger   I don't need illustrations. I know where the bits go, thank you. Can we get back to the plot?

Joanna   You actually shouted that at the screen.

Roger   Every time I looked they were at it. Without the sex, the story would have lasted about twenty minutes.

Joanna   Jenny said she and Chris watched the first episode and at the end, he turned it off and said, 'I don't think this is for us, dear.'

Roger   I'm with Chris. I hate watching soppy sex on television.

Joanna   I suppose you'd prefer to watch the news.

Roger   Might as well see what's going on in the world.

Joanna   The same stuff that was going on at lunchtime and on the *Today* programme this morning …

Roger   All right, just turn it off, then!

Joanna turns it off.

Joanna   Fine! Why do we always end up bickering about what to watch?

Roger   Because you can never make a decision.

Joanna   I'm generously offering *you* the option to choose!

Roger   But whatever I decide, you veto it!

Joanna   Because you mostly choose crap!

Roger   Thank you. Why don't you stomp off to bed?

Joanna   That's what you want, isn't it?

Roger   Well, I don't think the evening's going to end well if you hang about, seething.

Joanna   You want me out of the way so you can watch *Game of Thrones* for the hundredth time, don't you?

Roger   Not necessarily, but I wouldn't mind a bit of time to myself.

Joanna starts to storm off and calls back.

Joanna   Have all the time you like!

Roger   I will. Goodnight!

Joanna comes back again.

Joanna   What are you going to do?

Roger jumps.

Roger   Blimey! I thought you'd gone. I'll do whatever I want.

Joanna   And what is that?

Roger   Well, given a free choice, at this time of night, I'd find something that I know will relax me and make me smile, which is unlikely to be you at the moment.

Joanna   *Dad's Army*, I suppose?

Roger   That is certainly a possibility, but I think I've had enough TV for one night.

Joanna   Why don't you come to bed, then?

Roger   Not just yet.

Joanna   Are you going to read?

Roger   Probably not. Might pick my nose. Howl at the moon. Whatever floats my boat. What's it to you?

Joanna   Put the headphones on, if it's anything noisy.

Roger   Bit of radio, I think.

Joanna   The news headlines. I knew it!

Roger   No.

Joanna   What, then?

Roger   Why do you need to know? Are you going to censor my radio listening as well? Go to bed!

Joanna   Just tell me and I'll leave you in peace.

Roger   OK. *Round the Horne*.

Joanna   Oh, brilliant! Gorgeous idea. Shift up.

Roger   You said you were leaving me in peace.

Joanna   I lied.

Roger   I'd like to listen to it quietly. And alone.

Joanna   You don't mean that.

Roger   Would it make any difference if I did?

Joanna   None at all.

They both laugh.

MUSIC BREAK

Joybringer – Manfred Mann

SCENE 2: *Very early the following morning.*

Roger Stop bouncing around!

Joanna I'm awake.

Roger Then go back to sleep.

Joanna I've had enough sleep.

Roger Does that mean I've had enough sleep too? Just so I know.

Joanna You've got a very young back.

Roger Could you get fully awake before you start incoherent ramblings?

Joanna I mean it. No, don't turn round! I like looking at your back.

Roger Thank you. Can I turn round now?

Joanna Not yet. Remember when your hair got long and shaggy?

Roger Of course. I kept being told I looked like that French bloke on Netflix.

Joanna I just lay here thinking you could easily still be twenty-five … from behind.

Roger Was that when you jumped on me?

Joanna Quite often, yes.

Roger And when I turned round to face you and you said, 'Forget it, I'll make the tea.'

They laugh.

Roger I hated it long.

Joanna I know. You made me cut it.

Roger Oh and how I regretted that decision.

Joanna In hindsight, I probably shouldn't have used

Bonzo Dog's old grooming clippers.

Roger You think? I went from Mathias in *Call My Agent* to a Rikers Island inmate in ten minutes.

Joanna laughs.

Joanna I'd never seen you with a buzz cut.

Roger And never will again. I'm turning round now.

Joanna Me too.

Roger Oh, we're doing spoons, are we?

Joanna Do I have a nice back?

Roger Beautiful. Strong and sexy.

Joanna Do you sometimes lie there looking at my back?

Roger Endlessly. Especially when we're not speaking.

Joanna I think a bare back is very alluring, don't you?

Roger Yours certainly is.

Joanna As long as it's not spotty.

Roger That's a given.

Joanna I'm with Marilyn Monroe …

Roger A sentence I often say in my dreams.

Joanna All she ever wore in bed was Chanel Number 5.

Roger Must have made the sheets damp.

Joanna I just don't see any point in nightwear.

Roger That's because you're a shameless hussy.

Joanna I did buy you some posh silk pyjamas. Remember? After Toby was here on that very hot weekend?

Roger laughs.

Roger When he suddenly burst into our bedroom? Oh, yeah!

Joanna We'd flung off the sheets and were sprawled naked and entwined …

Roger And he said, 'I'm so sorry,' and fainted.

Joanna He was having a terrible nosebleed. That's why he came in to us – and why he passed out, obviously.

Roger You think that's why? I have my doubts.

They laugh.

Joanna I do love you in the mornings.

Roger Yes, you do. Frequently.

Joanna OK. So. Cup of tea, or what?

Roger Or what, I think …

Roger's phone rings.

Roger What the …? Who rings at this time in the morning?

Joanna Scammers? Wrong numbers? Australians?

Roger picks up the phone, yawning.

Roger And friends in need. It's Peter. [*talks into phone*] Hello, mate. How are you doing? Oh, right. Where are you? Ermm … I'm sure that'll be OK. Of course we don't mind … Peter? [*to Joanna*] Line's gone dead. He's in Carcassonne. Wants to come and stay for a few days.

Joanna Again? A few days turned into two weeks last time.

Roger I don't think he knows what to do with himself.

Joanna So he's still just wandering around, sobbing on friends' sofas?

Roger Getting dumped at the altar would knock most people sideways.

Joanna I know. Poor Peter. When's he coming?

Roger	Didn't get that far before the phone went dead. But I reckon in the next twenty-four hours. So I propose a spontaneous outing. Today. Sharpish.
Joanna	Why?
Roger	Because … there's nothing on TV? Why not?
Joanna	It's a bit … sudden. Couldn't we make it tomorrow?
Roger	Then it wouldn't be spontaneous, would it? Also, Peter will be probably be here by then.
Joanna	OK. Great. What shall we do?
Roger	This is what's happening. We'll make a day of it. Go into town, have coffee and croissants, take a walk by the river. Spot of lunch. Catch a movie matinee and then a drink and early supper at Villa Carlotta …
Joanna	That's very extravagant.
Roger	Not really. We hardly spent a penny last year – no holiday, no social life. Can't remember the last time we went to a restaurant.
Joanna	You're so masterful.
Roger	You can't say that any more. Smacks of patriarchy.
Joanna	All right, you're so bossy.
Roger	Enough of your insolence, woman! Run me a bath and fetch a warm sponge! [*his phone rings*] Ohhh … Peter again.
Joanna	Don't talk for long. Tell him you've got a hot date!

MUSIC BREAK
Everywhere – Fleetwood Mac

SCENE 3: *The kitchen, half an hour later. Joanna is eating a bit of toast. Roger enters, ready to go.*

Roger   Peter should get here sometime tomorrow, he thinks.

Joanna   Vague as ever.

Roger   Depends on flights.

Joanna   Did he say why he's coming?

Roger   He's just very upset. Kirsty and her new man Harry are planning to take the baby to Canada.

Joanna   Doesn't he have any say in that?

Roger   That's what he's trying to find out. What are you doing?

Joanna   Just having a quick bit of toast.

Roger   We're going out for breakfast!

Joanna   I know. But I was peckish. By the time we get into town, I'll be really hungry again. Promise.

Roger   Let's go, then.

Joanna   Just got to put the washing on.

Roger   Do it when we get back.

Joanna   Don't be daft! It won't take a minute. Did you say you wanted your blue chinos washed?

Roger   Yes. But no urgency.

Joanna   Nip up and get them.

Roger   Must I?

Joanna   Of course. No point in doing half a load.

Roger   If we don't leave by half past …

Joanna   We will. If you stop talking and go and get them.

Roger goes. Joanna's phone rings.

Joanna   Oh, hi, Aubrey! Have you? Oh, that's super! Erm …

Could you make it tomorrow instead? Oh, Dubai.
That's nice. Won't it? Well, OK. Yes, that'll be fine.
Thanks. Bye.

Joanna ends call. Roger enters. Hands her his chinos.

Roger   Here you are. Can we go now?

Joanna   That was Aubrey on the phone.

Roger   The plumber?

Joanna   He's got the new soft-close loo seat for the en
suite.

Roger   That's excellent news.

Joanna   And he says he wants to fit it.

Roger   Good. I'd rather he did it than me.

Joanna   So he's coming round.

Roger   When?

Joanna   In half an hour.

Roger   Didn't you tell him we're going out?!

Joanna   I asked him if he could come tomorrow but he's
off to Dubai.

Roger   We'll wait till he gets back.

Joanna   No! We can't live with the wobbly old seat any
longer. And he's going for a month. His daughter
lives there.

Roger   It's messing up all our plans.

Joanna   I couldn't say no. We've been waiting ages. He's so
much in demand and he said it won't take more
than half an hour.

Roger   Put some more toast on, then. We'll skip breakfast
in town and just go for lunch, before the film.

Joanna   And we'll still have all day, won't we?

MUSIC BREAK
Days – The Kinks

SCENE 4: *The kitchen, two hours later. Joanna is talking to Sally on the phone.*

Joanna   No, I can't do lunch, Sal. Sorry. It would have been good. But I'm … Especially as what? What garden? When? But we're going into town, to see a movie. Is he? Did I? Oh, that was before … No, it's OK. If he's got all the plants. Yes, I will. Better go. Talk later. Bye, Sal …

Roger enters.

Roger   Right. I've just settled up with Aubrey. Come on, we might just get in a brisk stroll along the riverbank before lunch.

Joanna   Ted's on his way over.

Roger   Sally's Ted? Why?

Joanna   You remember he said he'd landscape the border for us, when we had supper the other night?

Roger   Don't tell me. You told him Wednesday would be fine.

Joanna   I must have done. I don't remember saying it but of course it didn't matter, because we didn't have any plans at the time.

Roger   So have you just remembered?

Joanna   Sally phoned to suggest she and I had lunch while Ted sorted out the garden. I said, 'What garden?'

Roger   OK, so has she phoned him? Told him not to come?

Joanna	We can't stop him. He's stacked the van with all sorts of plants and stuff. He's doing us a favour.
Roger	By screwing up our day out?
Joanna	It's not his fault!
Roger	All right. All is not lost. We can show him where everything is and leave him to it. Can't we?
Joanna	It's not ideal. He'll want to talk us through the design and get our opinion.
Roger	It's nearly lunchtime!
Joanna	I know. [*mutters guiltily*] I said I'd make sandwiches.
Roger	For him?
Joanna	For all of us.
Roger	But we're supposed to be having lunch out!
Joanna	What's more important? A lunch out or getting the garden sorted?
Roger	It's not either/or. We can get the garden sorted another day!
Joanna	But it's Ted's day off from the garden centre and he's kindly spending it working here, as a friend.
Roger	This is ridiculous. No wonder we're in a rut.
Joanna	What does that mean?
Roger	You were complaining we were boring and, as always, I took immediate steps to prove you wrong. Instantly planning a day out, a terrific film, a delicious Italian supper … What could possibly go wrong? Pretty much every bloody thing!
Joanna	I'm sorry. But we can still see the film. We can talk to Ted while we have sandwiches and then, yes, we can leave him to it. Oh. Just had a thought …

	It's going to be awkward with Peter here, if Ted's doing our garden.
Roger	Why? Peter knows Sally's with Ted. He doesn't mind.
Joanna	He didn't mind when he was with Kirsty and the baby and they were getting married. But she's walked out on him now, so …
Roger	You think he wants to stay with us so he's near Sally?
Joanna	I don't know but I wouldn't be at all surprised. He's obviously in a state. And I know he misses the dog.
Roger	Did you tell Sally Peter's coming to stay?
Joanna	She'll find out soon enough. Probably tomorrow. I bet he phones her straight away …

Roger's phone honks with a text message.

Joanna	Peter again?
Roger	[*cagey*] No.
Joanna	Who is it?
Roger	It's … just someone.
Joanna	Who?!
Roger	The wine merchants.
Joanna	Why are they texting you? Special offers?
Roger	It seems we have a delivery arriving between fourteen thirty and eighteen thirty.
Joanna	Which you forgot about?
Roger	It needs to be signed for.

Joanna barely suppresses a laugh.

Roger	Don't say anything!

Joanna I'll just put the washing in the dryer, shall I?
Roger I can hear you smirking!

MUSIC BREAK

Here I Go Again – The Hollies

SCENE 5: *Two hours later. Roger is in the kitchen. Joanna storms in from the garden and slams the door.*

Roger You should have come in before it started raining.
Joanna is angry.
Joanna I certainly should.
Roger Do you want a cup of tea?
Joanna No, thanks. Where were you? You said you were going to help.
Roger I told you, I had to put all the wine away first.
Joanna I needed you.
Roger I thought you and Ted could manage. I'm sorry I wasn't there.
Joanna I'm sorry you weren't there, too. Very sorry.
Roger OK. I'm coming out to help now!
Joanna Don't bother.
Roger What?!
Joanna Something nasty happened in the hut.
Roger Don't you mean 'the woodshed', Ada Doom?
Joanna It's not funny.
Roger All right. What happened in the woodshed – the hut?
Joanna When the rain started, I was coming in but Ted suggested we dive in the hut and sort out the plants.

247

Roger   The bounder!

Joanna   Stop it.

Roger   Sorry. Go on.

Joanna   And then it started. A Grade-A, full-on, classic pervy pass.

Roger   He made a pass at you?! What did he say?

Joanna   We were talking about slugs and rabbits. Don't make a joke …!

Roger   I wasn't going to.

Joanna   And how to deter them. He said he loved a raised bed because – and I quote – 'It's very satisfying, moving things around in the bed until you achieve the desired result. Without having to bend over.'

Roger   Isn't that true?

Joanna   Then he started planting out the big terracotta tub and said, 'I just love getting my hands deep down and dirty.'

Roger   That's the sort of thing gardeners are always saying.

Joanna   He added, 'I've got a feeling you like dirty hands, too.'

Roger   Couldn't he have just been sharing his technique for working the soil? Gardeners get very excited about textures.

Joanna   Oh, for God's sake! Don't you think I know the difference between a Monty Don tutorial and a come-on?

Roger   He wasn't joking?

Joanna   No, he wasn't!

Roger leaps into action.

Roger   Right! Where is he?

Joanna   It's OK. It's sorted.

Roger   How? What happened?

Joanna   Well, first of all, I laughed in his face because it was so … Benny Hill … and then I said, 'You're going out with my best friend,' and he said, 'I know but I've always fancied you.' Then I asked, 'So what do you think's going to happen next?' And he said, 'I know what I'd like to happen …'

Roger   Jeez, what a creep!

Joanna   Exactly. So I said, 'But here's what will *actually* happen. You will go back to Sally and tell her what you just said to me, OK?' He shrugged and said, 'But it was just a bit of fun.' I said, 'It certainly wasn't fun. It was offensive, pathetic and extremely bad manners and if you don't tell Sally, I will tell her. Those are the only two options.'

Roger   So is he cowering in the hut?

Joanna   He's gone.

Roger   Where?

Joanna   I don't know. I don't care. He wimped off. Never to be seen again, I hope. On the plus side, he left all the supplies and plants and a very decent strimmer.

Roger   You're very calm.

Joanna   I'm not. [*seething*] I'm very cross. We'll have to get another gardener … Maybe Peter can give us a hand?

Roger   He's a bit limp and weepy at the moment.

Joanna   That's more use than a predatory scumbag.

Roger   God, I wish I'd come out earlier!

Joanna   So do I. Although it's good I found out what he's really like. But poor Sally. First Peter dumps her and now this slimeball.

Roger   Will you really tell her what happened, if he doesn't?

Joanna   I certainly will. I can't let her carry on believing he's a keeper. Now I need a bath. I feel dirty, and not in a good way.

Roger is quite upset.

Roger   The arrogance of thinking he could seduce you – while I was just yards away! God, it could have gone badly wrong. He's a big, powerful bloke.

Joanna   But I was leaning on the shovel. Which I was quite prepared to swing at him.

Roger   You weren't scared?

Joanna   What?! No! I'm very, very angry. For Sally, mostly. How dare he cheat on her?

Roger   I'm sorry you had to go through that.

Joanna   I'll survive. Why don't we go out tonight? We've missed the matinee but we can still make supper at Villa Carlotta! You've booked a table, haven't you?

Roger   Certainly have. You sure you feel like it?

Joanna   Of course I jolly well do!

Roger gets a text.

Joanna   Don't tell me – Peter?

Roger   'Fraid so. He's got an early flight. He'll be here about eight tonight.

Joanna Did he ask if we were busy? Or going out? At all?

Roger No, he didn't.

Joanna Well, I don't want to rush home by eight. Text him back and say we're out and we won't be home till late. He can sit on the doorstep. Or we'll leave a key.

Roger No. I know when I'm beaten. I'm not making any more arrangements for anyone ever again. We'll get a takeaway. Watch TV –

Joanna For a change.

Roger – till he gets here.

Joanna Why does everyone seem to think we're always at home? Sitting around doing nothing so they can drop in at any time?

Roger Maybe word's got round that we're stuck in a rut?

MUSIC BREAK

Stuck in the Middle with You – Stealers Wheel

SCENE 6: *The garden, four days later. Roger's planting out. Joanna arrives.*

Joanna Hi! Oh, those look nice. But isn't it a bit early to put them out? There might be a frost.

Roger Let's be optimistic and assume there won't be.

Joanna Shouldn't the tall ones go behind?

Roger They *are* going behind. I haven't put them in properly yet.

Joanna I can see that. Don't forget to water them.

Roger What's the matter with you? Someone drain the swimming pool?

Joanna No. But there were a lot of walruses wallowing up and down and blocking the lanes. I did eventually say to one, 'This is the fast lane.' And he said, 'Yes, that's why I'm in it.' Lardy bloater!

Roger I'm so glad the swim relaxed you and you came back a nicer person.

Joanna Sorry. It's been an exhausting week, hasn't it? Peter dripping around and Sally sobbing over Ted.

Roger The sobbing soon stopped when you told her he'd tried to chat you up.

Joanna I shouldn't have had to but when I found out he'd said he was leaving because he was 'frightened he was falling too deeply in love with her', I just lost it. I felt really bad but it does help that Peter's here. He's been seeing quite a bit of her.

Roger He's round there all the bloody time! He's supposed to be helping me with the garden!

Joanna I think Sally needs him more than you do. Oh, guess what? We're on our own tonight!

Roger Wow! First time for a week.

Joanna Sally's asked him over for supper. So you don't have to cook for three.

Roger Oh, I'm cooking tonight again, am I?

Joanna You said you got those smoked crevettes and some samphire …

Roger	I have. And they'd be wasted on Peter, who's a KFC account holder.
Joanna	Well, I'll appreciate them. So. It'll just be us. On our own. Oh, wait. I've got Pilates at six.
Roger	Here we go.
Joanna	But it's only an hour. I'll come home, put a floaty frock on. Light some candles …
Roger	While I slave away in the kitchen?
Joanna	You know you love it.
Roger	A romantic supper for two. Mmmm … who can I ask?
Joanna	Funny. What are you going to cook?
Roger	For starters, the crevettes don't need cooking. Pasta puttanesca to follow?
Joanna	Lovely.
Roger	And would madam consider baked peaches and crème fraiche an acceptable pud?
Joanna	Most acceptable. Thank you. I'm excited! It'll be like a date … I'll be feminine and fluttery and you'll be attentive and pull the chair out for me …
Roger	Want me to peel your prawns as well?
Joanna	No. But you can spoon feed me peaches.
Roger	Where're you going?
Joanna	Indoors. It's starting to rain again. Why?
Roger	Can you help me shift these pots first?

MUSIC BREAK
Flowers in the Rain – The Move

SCENE 7: *8.30 p.m. Joanna and Roger have just finished supper at home. Joanna sighs.*

Joanna Your peaches were perfect.

Roger Seconds? Oh, no, you've had those. Thirds?

Joanna I know when I've had enough.

Roger Hah! You don't!

Joanna What do you think Peter and Sally are up to?

Roger They're probably taking the dog round the block.

Joanna They were so perfect together but I can't see it happening again.

Roger Why not?

Joanna Too much has gone on. Peter's had a child and Sally's got more independent. They've both changed.

Roger Well, that's good, isn't it? They've had a few life experiences but maybe they've discovered that they want to be together. Again.

Joanna But they've been apart for nearly three years!

Roger Same as us. We split up a few times and got back together. Once, after nearly three years.

Joanna Yes, of course. That incredibly hot summer of seventy-six.

Roger Should have been a fantastic time for us. You had a terrific job at the publishers and I was ...

Joanna You were restless.

Roger So were you. It had been a tough year. We'd finally learned that there was no way we could be parents.

254

Joanna   And all our friends seemed to be pushing out babies like exploding popcorn.

Roger   And asking us to be godparents.

Joanna   I wanted to scream, 'No! I don't think your baby is the most beautiful in the world. He's nowhere near as gorgeous as mine — ours — would have been!'

Small silence.

Joanna   Sorry.

Roger   We should have sat down and talked about it properly.

Joanna   Nobody did therapy in those days.

Roger   So we just accelerated apart.

Joanna   Accelerated?

Roger   Well, what would you call it? It was a lot faster than drifting.

Joanna   We were both really busy.

Roger   But most evenings, we headed off in opposite directions. You had to see a play or an author's lecture. And I had to …

Joanna   Yes, what did you do, every night?

Roger   You never asked me. Weren't interested.

Joanna   I probably didn't care.

Roger   It was a pretty sociable time, in Fleet Street and around Soho. Lots of mates …

Joanna   Drinking buddies?

Roger   Some of them were proper friends, like John.

Joanna   Lovely John. I do miss him.

Roger   He was definitely one of the good guys. I'd seen

       him that night.

Joanna   The night you decided to leave me.

Roger   I hadn't decided anything but I knew we couldn't
       continue as we were.

Joanna   I was quite surprised when you suggested we
       meet in town and actually go home together.

Roger   I walked across Trafalgar Square and – I can see
       you now – you were sitting by the fountain, with
       your feet in the water …

Joanna   It was the hottest night of the year.

Roger   You were wearing that beaded vintage jacket,
       white T-shirt, denim skirt.

Joanna   I'd been to a works party, I think.

Roger   A policeman was standing over you.

Joanna   He came up to tell me off for paddling but we got
       chatting. He said did I see Justin Hayward walk
       past. He was a great fan of the Moody Blues but
       didn't like to ask for his autograph when he was
       on duty. I offered to do it for him but then you
       arrived …

Roger   I had been watching you for a long time.

Joanna   That's why you were late.

Roger   You looked … happy, swishing your feet about.

Joanna   I'm always happy when I'm near water.

Roger   And I thought, 'I'm not making her happy.'

Joanna   Perhaps I was looking happy because I was going
       to meet you.

Roger   Were you?

Joanna   I don't remember. But I do remember you just

came and sat beside me and took off your shoes
and we both had our feet in the water, not
looking at each other, and I thought, 'Something's
going to happen.' I didn't know what it was but I
felt strangely ... calm.

Roger I had this speech prepared. I wrote some notes.

Joanna It sounded like you'd spent some time working
on it. It was quite formal. You didn't look at me,
you just said, 'There are people who are very
important at different times in our lives. But not
everyone is for ever.' I thought you were going to
tell me you were having an affair.

Roger That would have been easy. This was much
tougher.

Joanna You spoke very seriously. 'You fall in love and
you're happy – and you can't imagine it will ever
end ...' Then a pigeon landed beside you and you
started talking to it, instead of me.

Roger Because I couldn't really look at you.

Joanna You looked as if you were in pain.

Roger I was.

Joanna You said, 'Time passes and one of you – maybe
both of you – starts to feel you must've had the
best of times ...'

Roger '... because it sure doesn't feel like the best of
times any more.'

Joanna And then the pigeon crapped. And it should have
been funny and normally we would have laughed
together but we didn't laugh. You just carried on

        talking …

Roger I had to get to the end. What I wanted to say was, 'But you hold on, because if there's a chance, a tiny chance that it will get better by itself and you'll love each other again, you want to grab that chance. You don't want to hear the words, "I'm leaving you."'

Joanna So you said it first. You took away the possibility of hearing those words from me, by saying them yourself.

Roger I didn't actually say I was leaving you …

Joanna You said you were going to Chicago.

Roger John had put in a word for me. The university were looking for a visiting lecturer.

Joanna I was amazed because you'd said you didn't like being a lecturer and you were going back to journalism.

Roger But it seemed absolutely the right thing to do at the time. You could have come with me.

Joanna You didn't ask me.

Roger You didn't say you wanted me to ask you. I think we both knew that it had to happen like it did.

Joanna Funnily enough, we went home holding hands. We got on better that night than we had for months.

Roger Didn't seem real. I felt I was looking down on someone else.

Joanna Till you left, we were behaving more like brother and sister. Being very careful with each other.

Roger   It was so hard. Many times, I almost begged you to stay with me. But I didn't.

Joanna   Many times I wanted you to. But we're both too stubborn to grovel. I couldn't believe it was happening, but you were right. We were not good to each other then. I certainly wasn't good for you. We'd been together for nearly seven years. I thought it was maybe just that famous 'itch'.

Roger   I really felt it was The End. But I left because you seemed to be OK.

Joanna   Honestly, I didn't miss you that much at first.

Roger   I was pretty busy too.

Joanna   The flat was tidy and quiet. I got a cat. Do you remember?

Roger   Surprising, as you're a dog person.

Joanna   I suppose if it happened now, we'd be Zooming and FaceTiming and keeping in touch … There weren't even emails then.

Roger   The longer we left it, the more it became a past life.

Joanna   But you did come back.

Roger   The contract finished.

Joanna   You arrived in the middle of my birthday party.

Roger   Which I'd forgotten.

Joanna   But you bought me a present. A Chicago White Sox baseball jacket.

Roger   I knew you liked Americana.

Joanna   I just stared at you and you fell to your knees and said, 'I knew it! You'd have preferred the New

York Giants!'

Roger   I never did get presents right.

Joanna   That made me laugh. Everybody was so pleased to see you. Hugs all round.

Roger   Except for you. You were quite brisk and jolly.

Joanna   I was trying to hold it together till everyone had gone. Except you started to leave as well.

Roger   I was just another guest. I didn't want to stand around like a needy drip.

Joanna   Were you glad when I made you stay?

Roger   It wasn't a romantic moment. You just said, 'As we're selling the flat there's some stuff you've got to sign.'

Joanna   And then I said, 'Are you going away again?' And you said, 'Depends.'

Roger   I should have added 'On you' but I wasn't that confident. I was also jet-lagged.

Joanna   Tell me again your real reason for coming back? I like to hear you say it.

Roger   Forgotten.

Joanna   No you haven't.

Roger pours some more wine.

Roger   I need another drink first.

Joanna   We were sitting on the floor, going through the paperwork, and you just looked at me and started to smile. Then you said …

Roger   'I have a feeling you're going to grow older in a very interesting and wonderful way and I want to be there to see it.'

Joanna No one has ever said anything lovelier than that in the whole world.

Roger But I was so wrong! Look at you! A stooped, toothless crone – fag on, carpet slippers, shabby old dressing gown!

Joanna You can talk! Grumpy old git with a dodgy knee and a terrible taste in TV shows.

Roger That much is true. But I was right about you. Still dazzling. I'm glad I came back.

Joanna You've pulled. Race you upstairs!

A text comes through.

Roger Put the brakes on. I bet this is Peter saying he's on his way back.

Joanna No. It's my phone. It's Sally. 'Don't wait up. Peter's staying over and I haven't even shaved my legs but fortunately, he knows me so well. Thank God for familiar territory!'

Roger The old ones are the best.

Joanna Are you talking about jokes or women?

Roger I'm talking about marriages.

Joanna Do you think Peter and Sally will grow old together?

Roger They already have. So have we.

Joanna I don't think we've changed at all. We still enjoy a frolic after a *lovely* dinner.

Roger We'd enjoy a frolic after *every* dinner, if it was down to you.

Joanna I hope that will still be true in ten, even twenty years.

261

Roger Some things will have to change – even for us.

Joanna Are you thinking hot chocolate and separate beds?

Roger Good grief, no!

Joanna What then?

Roger Well, when we're in our late eighties, I doubt the foreplay will include 'Race you upstairs'.

They laugh.

Joanna OK … So … Imagine we're octogenarians, how are you going to entice me to bed?

Roger Easy. Hey, baby! Fire up the Stannah, we're taking a stairlift to heaven!

They laugh.

END MUSIC
Time After Time – Matt Monro

Acknowledgements

Huge thanks to Profile Books for your enthusiasm, profession-alism and generosity. From the moment of Rebecca Gray's first call to say that she had listened to – and loved - *Conversations from a Long Marriage* on Radio 4 and 'Can we talk?', edits and emails from each and every individual have always been sprinkled with warm and complimentary messages; it's been an absolute joy.

Enormous gratitude to Sioned Wiliam, Julia McKenzie and Richard Morris at BBC Radio for embracing and championing the revolutionary concept of music, laughter and passion in a long marriage and for commissioning five series (so far).

Special love and thanks to Joanna Lumley and Roger Allam – this writer's dream team – who created a magical partner-ship which enhanced every line and brought my words hilar-iously to life, and producer Claire Jones, who somehow man-aged to harness the merry chaos of the recording studio into a comedy series which fills me with happiness and pride.

Finally, love to my husband, wonderful children, grand-children, my sisters, my very good friends and the radio audience, whose own conversations and messages inspire and entertain me every day.

About the Author

Jan Etherington is an award-winning British writer, journalist and broadcaster. For over thirty years she has been writing hit radio and TV comedy series with her husband (of almost forty years) and writing partner, Gavin Petrie. *Conversations from a Long Marriage*, originally on Radio 4, is her first solo narrative comedy. It won Best Radio Comedy in 2020 at the Voice of the Listener and Viewer Awards, and was nominated for the same in 2022 at the Writers' Guild Awards. The fifth series will begin in early 2024.